"I need your help. You can provide me with a legitimate cover for my investigation."

"How can I do that?" she protested. "I'm totally inexperienced, and it will take time for me to make any changes at the company. You would stick out like a sore thumb if I tried right off to put you in any kind of position at Horizon Pharmaceuticals."

"I know. That's why we'd have to arrange something different. I'll need a cover that will give me intimate access to the workings of the company."

The steadiness of his gaze told Carolyn that he had already decided what that cover should be. She felt a strange quiver in her stomach.

"When you arrive at Horizon for the first time, Carolyn, I need to be there with you—as your husband."

She choked on her intake of breath. "My husband?"

"In name only," he hastened to reassure her. "Don't you see? It's the perfect cover."

Dear Harlequin Intrigue Reader,

This month Harlequin Intrigue has an enthralling array of breathtaking romantic suspense to make the most of those last lingering days of summer.

The wait is finally over! The next crop of undercover agents who belong to the newest branch of the top secret Confidential organization are about to embark on an unbelievable adventure. Award-winning reader favorite Gayle Wilson will rivet you with the launch book of this brand-new ten-story continuity series. COLORADO CONFIDENTIAL will begin in Harlequin Intrigue, break out into a special release anthology and finish in Harlequin Historicals. In *Rocky Mountain Maverick*, an undeniably sexy undercover agent infiltrates a powerful senator's ranch and falls under the influence of an intoxicating impostor. Be there from the very beginning!

The adrenaline rush continues in *The Butler's Daughter* by Joyce Sullivan, with the first book in her new miniseries, THE COLLINGWOOD HEIRS. A beautiful guardian has been entrusted with the care of a toddler-sized heir, but now they are running for their lives and she must place their safety in an enigmatic protector's tantalizing hands! Ann Voss Peterson heats things up with *Incriminating Passion* when a targeted "witness" to a murder manages to inflame the heart of a by-the-book assistant D.A.

Finally rounding out the month is *Semiautomatic Marriage* by veteran author Leona Karr. Will the race to track down a killer culminate in a *real* trip down the aisle for an undercover husband and wife?

So pick up all four of these pulse-pounding stories and end the summer with a bang!

Sincerely,

Denise O'Sullivan
Harlequin Intrigue, Senior Editor

SEMIAUTOMATIC MARRIAGE

LEONA KARR

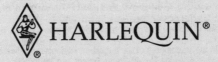

TORONTO • NEW YORK • LONDON
AMSTERDAM • PARIS • SYDNEY • HAMBURG
STOCKHOLM • ATHENS • TOKYO • MILAN • MADRID
PRAGUE • WARSAW • BUDAPEST • AUCKLAND

ISBN 0-373-22724-8

SEMIAUTOMATIC MARRIAGE

This edition published by arrangement with Harlequin Books S.A.

® and TM are trademarks of the publisher. Trademarks indicated with
® are registered in the United States Patent and Trademark Office, the
Canadian Trade Marks Office and in other countries.

Visit us at www.eHarlequin.com

Printed in U.S.A.

ABOUT THE AUTHOR

A native of Colorado, Leona (Lee) Karr is the author of nearly forty books. Her favorite genres are romantic suspense and inspirational romance. After graduating from the University of Colorado with a B.A. and the Univer-sity of Northern Colorado with an M.A., she taught as a reading specialist until her first book was published in 1980. She has been on the Waldenbooks bestseller list and nominated by *Romantic Times* for Best Romantic Saga and Best Gothic Author. She has been honored as the Rocky Mountain Fiction Writer of the Year, and received Colorado's Romance Writer of the Year award. Her books have been reprinted in more than a dozen foreign countries. She is a presenter at numerous writing conferences and has taught college courses in creative writing.

Books by Leona Karr

Don't miss any of our special offers. Write to us at the following address for information on our newest releases.

Harlequin Reader Service
U.S.: 3010 Walden Ave., P.O. Box 1325, Buffalo, NY 14269
Canadian: P.O. Box 609, Fort Erie, Ont. L2A 5X3

HORIZON PHARMACEUTICAL COMPANY

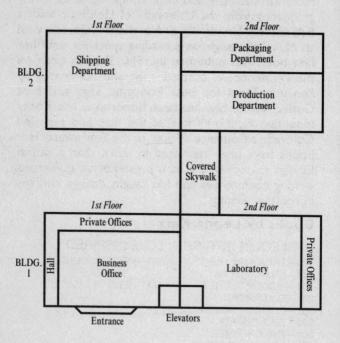

CAST OF CHARACTERS

Carolyn Leigh—A visit to a lawyer's office makes her an heiress and a partner in a dangerous charade.

Adam Lawrence—A man on a mission, who will use his status as a "pretend husband" to carry out his plan.

Jasper Stanford—A newly found relative who has little interest in being an uncle or friend.

Della Denison—An executive who seems willing to preserve her position at all costs. Her daughter, Lisa, is a spoiled young woman who lives a pampered life. Her son, Buddy, shows little interest in anything but pursuing his idle hobbies.

Cliff Connors—An assistant laboratory assistant who has an unsavory past that threatens to endanger the present.

Nick Calhoun—A man with a gambling habit.

Susan Kimble—A woman dedicated to her job and searching for happiness.

Nellie Ryan—A woman in love with a man who only brings trouble into her life.

Love and thanks to my sons, Leonard and Clark,
for their valuable help with this book,
and to Cindy Karr for her supportive interest
and encouragement.

Chapter One

Carolyn Leigh's eyes rounded as she looked at the two men seated across the table from her in the lawyer's office. "I thought this meeting was about my unknown benefactor, who's helped me financially through medical school, using your firm as a conduit."

"Well, in a way it is," the gray-haired lawyer, Mr. Bancroft, assured her as he pushed his glasses farther up his nose.

"Am I expected to pay it back?" she asked evenly, trying to keep the apprehension out of her voice. What she didn't need was more indebtedness. After having just graduated a month ago, she was trying to find a full-time medical position as soon as possible to alleviate her other debts.

"No, the grant was yours, free and clear," the lawyer assured her. "The news we have for you is good."

Carolyn tensed. *Good news?* Growing up as a sickly foster child, her life had been filled with people telling her they had good news for her, when the truth was she was just being shifted from one unsatisfactory foster placement to another. Even though she was an adult now, and had managed to get herself through medical school by sheer grit, and working a job for nearly six years, a remembered anxiety suddenly tightened her stomach. She still had nightmares about being helpless as a foster child, thrown into one traumatic experience after another. She'd felt like a pawn in some diabolical game. *Here we go again,* she thought, trying to steel herself for whatever was about to crash into her well-laid plans.

From the first moment Carolyn walked into the office, she'd sensed a certain hesitancy, as if the two men weren't exactly sure how to proceed. She'd only met William Bancroft, the elderly lawyer, once before, and had never met the good-looking, younger one, Adam Lawrence—Bancroft introduced him only by name, without identifying who he was and why he was there. She assumed he was a junior associate.

They politely offered her coffee, which she refused.

"Well, then, why don't you lay the groundwork, Adam?" Bancroft suggested, nodding at him. "We'll cover the legal details after that."

The dark-haired man smiled at her, and she was aware of his strong features, slightly tanned complexion and the determined jut of his chin. Somewhere in his thirties, he must have been, and his clear, gray-blue eyes narrowed slightly as if he were searching for the right way to begin. Carolyn's heartbeat suddenly quickened as she waited for Adam Lawrence to speak. What was this all about?

"You've heard of Arthur Stanford," he began in

a conversational tone, and smiled, as if he recognized her tenseness.

"No, I haven't," she answered with her usual honesty.

He seemed a little surprised at her directness. "Have you heard of Horizon Pharmaceuticals?"

"Of course. Everyone in the medical field is aware of Horizon. It's a major supplier of pharmaceutical drugs. One of the oldest companies in the Northwest, I believe."

He nodded. "That's right. Arthur Stanford is the owner of Horizon Pharmaceutical. He passed away recently."

"And there's some reason I should know this?" This man's death had probably been in the news, but she'd been too busy studying to read the newspaper. Something about this whole meeting put her on the defensive. There was an undercurrent in the room she didn't understand. Was she on the hot seat for some unknown reason? Plenty of schoolyard scuffles had conditioned her to get her mitts up before an expected blow came. She mentally geared up to be ready to handle whatever he was about to lay on her.

"The financial aid you've been receiving for medical school came from Arthur Stanford. He arranged for the grant to be paid through Mr. Bancroft's office."

"Really?" she answered in honest surprise.

"Yes, really."

She'd often wondered who'd set up the grant that had made it possible for her to attend medical school without interruption. She'd assumed that it was an organization, not an individual. The truth was, she'd applied for every financial aid listed in the college office. No one was more surprised than she was when the university's director of admissions called and told her that she'd been selected by an anonymous donor for a generous stipend.

"I've been very grateful for his financial help," she readily admitted. "It would have taken me an extra two years to work my way through medical school without it. My grant was a great deal more generous than most awards. Did Mr. Stanford financially help many medical students?"

"No, you're the only one."

"The only one?" she repeated in disbelief. "But why? I mean, why was I the fortunate one?"

Adam hesitated, not at all certain how to proceed. Bancroft had insisted that he be the one to tell her the truth, and he'd readily agreed, but Dr. Carolyn Leigh wasn't at all what he'd expected. By any standard, she was a very attractive woman: petite features, soft, shapely mouth, large, sky blue eyes and blond hair the color of rich honey. Even her simple, inexpensive pink summer blouse and navy skirt couldn't detract from a slender, shapely body that could easily give any man ideas.

Even though Adam had only been in her presence a few minutes, he'd already recognized that there was more to her than her appealing looks. An undeniable toughness and resilience radiated from her. He'd bet she could put any leering male in his place with a sharp word or a well-aimed kick. It wasn't hard for him to imagine her in a doctor's white jacket, a stethoscope around her neck and a bedside manner that could either charm or deftly manage the most unruly patient. No, she wasn't at all what he'd expected. He wondered if they were handling this all wrong. There was nothing to do now but plunge ahead and be as honest as he could.

"It wasn't an accident that you received the generous stipend," he explained. "You see, Carolyn, Arthur Stanford has a personal interest in you."

"How could that be? I told you I didn't know Arthur Stanford," she replied firmly. "I've never heard his name, as far as I know. And I have no reason to believe he'd have a special interest in me."

Clearly she wasn't about to accept the truth until she had more facts to back it up. Adam suspected this strong fiber in her personality was going to play havoc with his plans. He tried to keep his tone neutral, as if they were discussing something that wasn't going to change her life forever.

"It's true, isn't it, Carolyn, that you've grown up without family and without knowing who abandoned you as an infant?"

She nodded. Her unknown roots had been like an albatross around her neck since she was old enough to know what the word *orphan* meant. She'd always been treated like a changeling, not belonging anywhere, not to anyone. She'd learned very young to make her way in the world alone, and as far as she was concerned that wasn't going to change.

"I don't see why my background is of interest here." She firmed her chin as she locked her gaze on him. "What is this about?"

"I know that what I'm going to tell you, Carolyn, will be a shock. I guess there's no way to prepare you for the news, so I'll just come right out and say it." Adam had the foolish urge to reach out and hold her hand, but realized she'd reject the gesture. "Arthur Stanford had a very personal interest in you, Carolyn, because he was your grandfather."

Grandfather. The word exploded in Carolyn's head like a grenade. She tried to say something, but for once in her life, her mouth wouldn't work. Almost instantly shock turned into disbelief. It wasn't true. It couldn't be. With great effort, she found her voice.

"Let me get this straight. You're telling me that the money I've been receiving is from Arthur Stanford and he's my grandfather?"

He nodded. "That's exactly what I'm telling you. There's no doubt about it. You're Arthur Stanford's granddaughter."

Her whole life, Carolyn had dreamed of belonging to someone of her own flesh and blood, longing to know what family genes she carried. She'd fought all her battles from a sense of aloneness, and as she looked into Adam's reassuring face and gentle eyes, she pleaded silently, *Please, let this be true.*

He must have read the plea in her expression, because he smiled and took her hand. The warm contact gave her the reassurance she needed to believe the impossible.

"I have a complete report here," Bancroft said, handing Carolyn a folder.

Both men fell silent as she read the file.

For the first time Carolyn learned the mystery of her birth. Her mother, Alicia Stanford, had been a sixteen-year-old who ran away when she discovered she was pregnant. Her affluent family's efforts to find her ended unhappily a year later when she returned home with a terminal disease. She refused to say what had happened to the baby and would not identify the father. Apparently nothing was done to try to locate the baby until a few years ago.

Carolyn learned that she was just starting medical school when the investigators her widowed grandfather hired finally tracked her down, and the millionaire began to support her education.

"He knew for four years that I was his granddaughter!" Disbelief gave way to deep disappointment. Tears threatened to spill from her eyes. "Why didn't he tell me? Why did he keep it from me?"

"We don't know," the lawyer admitted. "When your grandfather arranged for your financial grant, he insisted on total secrecy."

"He received continuous updates about you," Adam told her. "He knew that you went to work for the financial firm Champion Realty and Investments right out of high school and could have worked your way up in that company. From all the reports, Carolyn, you certainly could have a career in business, as well as medicine."

Bancroft shoved his glasses up his nose and cleared his throat. "And that brings us to the legal matter at hand. The good news. The matter of his will."

Both men looked at her in a way that made her breath catch. "He left me…something?"

Adam couldn't resist a chuckle. "More than just something, I'd say."

Bancroft beamed. "Arthur Stanford made a new will just a few months before his death. Carolyn, you're the primary beneficiary."

The lawyer proceeded to inform her that Stanford had bequeathed her fifty-one percent of Horizon

Pharmaceuticals, his elegant mansion and other considerable monetary assets.

She stared at both men incredulously, her blue eyes rounding. What kind of macabre joke was this? She'd never been one to believe in fairy tales, and she certainly didn't believe in this one. It had to be a hoax! A cruel manipulation of some kind.

Seeing a red flush mounting her neck, Adam said quickly, "It's true, Carolyn. Your grandfather died several weeks ago, and all the legalities are settled. There were just a few necessary verifications to make before telling you."

"You're expecting me to believe that Arthur Stanford bypassed everyone else to leave a fortune to his long-lost granddaughter?"

"Yes, Carolyn, that's exactly what has happened."

"What about the other people in his life?" Carolyn demanded as a blessed logical detachment allowed her to get her emotions under control. She wanted facts. She wasn't about to accept anything at face value. Especially not a Cinderella story like the one they were trying to lay on her. "There were other people in his life, weren't there?"

"Yes," Bancroft answered readily. "There is one son, your mother's older brother, Jasper. He's mentioned in the will, but in a lesser way."

"Why would Arthur Stanford do that? I mean, I don't understand why he didn't leave his son the company and everything else."

Adam spoke up. "Maybe because Jasper ran two companies and property of his own into bankruptcy, and his father had to bail him out. Obviously Stanford didn't want the same thing to happen to Horizon.''

''And there's no one else?'' she asked with a dry mouth.

''No blood relation, other than Jasper. You're the only one,'' Bancroft answered. ''Jasper is a laboratory scientist at Horizon, and your grandfather left him some stock, but you hold the controlling interest. Jasper never married, but he has maintained a five-year romantic relationship with Della Denison, a very capable career woman, who also works at Horizon. They live in the Stanford mansion, along with Della's two children, both in their twenties.'' He paused. ''Apparently your grandfather found this arrangement amicable.''

''But it may not continue to be so when you take up residency there,'' Adam warned her. ''Remember, Carolyn, in the end you will be the one to decide if any changes need to be made. Everything has been put on hold since your grandfather's death.''

''Until all the legalities are finalized,'' Bancroft said, ''I can arrange for generous funds to be available to you to take care of your immediate financial needs.'' As he continued to expand on the details of the will, Carolyn's doubts began to fade, and a flood of questions took their place.

Adam leaned toward her and waited for her eyes to meet his before he said, ''It's important that I share some disturbing facts with you now, Carolyn, before you move into the role of a wealthy heiress.''

Heiress. The word lacked any meaning for her. She'd never had enough money to cover her monthly expenses. Her secondhand car had more than a hundred thousand miles on it. At the moment she was unemployed since no one had jumped at her résumé or brand-new medical degree.

"Your grandfather's death was a surprise to everyone," Adam told her. "Very unfortunate."

"Was he ill?" she asked, wishing she could have been at his side. Her medical training might have counted for something if she could have cared for him.

The way Carolyn's expectant gaze was fixed on him made Adam wish he had more than just empirical facts to tell her. He knew she was in for another shock. "No, it wasn't illness that ended his life. I'm sorry I have to tell you that your grandfather was a victim of a hit-and-run driver."

She stared at him, a sickening lump lodged in her throat. Maybe her grandfather *had* planned to reveal himself to her, but met an untimely death before it happened. She felt an even greater loss, knowing how he'd died.

"Stanford was killed in a waterfront location, and there seems to be some question whether his death was accidental."

At first his words refused to penetrate. Then she said in disbelief, "You mean someone deliberately hit him?"

"We don't know. That's why I'm here, Carolyn." He reached into his pocket and drew out a badge. "I'm a federal investigator, and among other things, I'm assigned to cover your grandfather's suspicious death."

"You're not a lawyer? I mean, I thought—"

"I work for the FDA. Mr. Bancroft asked me to be here because he knows I've been investigating

Arthur Stanford's affairs. Since you are his beneficiary, you'll be able to help me.''

''Help you? With what? I don't see—''

''You'll be in a position to look into every aspect of the company and have access to family affairs.''

She gave a shaky laugh as she shook her head. ''I have no idea what you have in mind, but I certainly need more time and information before I can handle any of this.'' She stood up. ''I'm sorry, gentlemen, but my head is reeling. You'll have to excuse me.''

''I know this is a lot to absorb in such a short time,'' Adam readily agreed. ''But time is of the utmost importance, Carolyn. I hate to pressure you, but...''

''I never make decisions under pressure. Whatever you have to say, Mr. Lawrence, will have to wait.'' She used her professional tone, masking the racing of her heart.

An heiress. A mansion. Horizon.

She gave them both a mechanical smile and hurriedly left the office. Maybe all this was on the up-and-up, but her emotions were in such a tangle at the moment she couldn't be sure. Could it really be that her grandfather had found her? She wanted to believe the unbelievable, but her intuition was quivering like an antenna trying to catch warning vibes. The handsome Adam Lawrence, obviously, wanted a commitment of some kind from her. What was his real agenda? Why had the lawyer included him in the meeting? There'd been moments she'd instinctively responded to his smile and the touch of his hand, but now she wondered if he'd been deliberately manipulating her emotions.

With her thoughts whirling like an off-center helicopter, she crossed the lot to her car, parked at the back of the small brick building. Her hands trembled as she unlocked the door of her old car. After sliding into the worn front seat, she sat there for a long minute. She needed to go home, go over all the legal papers again, get on the Internet and see what information she could pull up on Horizon Pharmaceuticals. As her analytical approach to problems settled her emotions, she turned the key in the ignition.

The engine refused to turn over. After repeated tries she slapped the steering wheel in exasperation. She'd been having trouble with it for more than a month, but had been trying to put off the expense of car repair as long as possible.

She silently swore and then tried again, but no luck. The irony of the situation hit her when she looked out the window and saw Adam Lawrence walking across the parking lot, heading for her car. It was obvious from his expression that he'd heard the starter grinding.

She had little choice but to roll down the window and nod at his friendly "Won't start, huh?"

His grin only made her feel more testy. *Brilliant deduction. Were all FDA agents so perceptive?*

"Would you like me to try?" he offered.

"Thanks, but don't bother." She didn't want to prolong the embarrassment. It didn't take a mechanic to know that the old car was heading for the junkyard. What to do now? Leave it? Take a bus home and see if her AAA insurance was still in force? "I think I'll just let it sit for a while."

"How about I run you home and you can call someone to look at it?"

"No need to put you to that trouble," she answered quickly.

"It's no trouble. Just tell me how to get there. I'm still trying to find my way around Seattle."

As she hesitated, he saw a flicker of indecision in her eyes. He could tell that she was tempted to accept his offer. The stalled car could be a blessing in disguise. Her sudden departure from the meeting had left him wondering how to initiate further contact with her. It was imperative to move quickly to enlist her help. He was relieved when she nodded.

As they walked to his car, he made an idle comment about the gathering rain clouds. "There's more rain here in a week than we have in a whole season back home."

"The natives call it liquid sunshine," she informed him with a faint smile.

"I grew up in New Mexico. Ever been there?" he asked, hoping to make the situation seem casual and friendly.

"No, but I don't think I'd like it," she said frankly. "I'd miss the water."

He could tell from her pensive expression that her thoughts were beyond any casual chitchat. Not that he could blame her. She'd been given a double whammy. Learning the identity of her grandfather would have been shock enough, but the inheritance on top of that would knock anyone for a loop. He knew from her case history that she possessed a dogged will that had obviously shaped her life. The vulnerable innocence about her was utterly deceptive. She wouldn't be easily persuaded to fall in line with his plans.

As she sat in the seat beside him, he was aware

of her appealing femininity, the lines and curves of her body. Her summer blouse molded the fullness of her breasts, and its open collar revealed the smooth lines of her neck. A faint floral scent teased his nostrils, and he realized that he'd been without feminine company far too long.

She told him the address of her apartment and gave him directions. He related a couple of humorous experiences he'd had trying to find his way in foreign countries and was rewarded with a slight smile.

"Have you traveled abroad quite a bit?" she asked.

"Not really. South America, mostly. I lived in Brazil for a couple of years. I served as the judicial attaché at the United States Embassy and coordinated evidence of drug-related activities."

"I see. And when you came back to the States, you became an FDA agent?"

"Yes."

As he fell silent, Carolyn was aware of the change in him. A shadow passed over his eyes, and she sensed that for some reason the subject was painful for him. What had happened in his career, she wondered, to put that kind of pain in his expression? She remembered how very intense he'd been in the lawyer's office. Obviously Bancroft had asked him to be there, and she had cut him off when he tried to explain his interest in her sudden legacy.

"Is this the place?" he asked as he pulled up in front of the large house owned by an elderly widow from whom she rented an upstairs apartment.

"Yes, this is…home." She hesitated slightly over the word as she reached for the door handle. She was still feeling overwhelmed, but a blessed detachment had begun to ease her bewilderment.

"Carolyn, could we talk a minute? I know your head must be swimming with all this, but I really need to share some things with you. Would you just hear me out? It's important. There are some decisions that have to be made."

"I'm not ready to make decisions of any kind," she answered firmly. "I've read about people who suddenly come into money and how they're hounded by the public, pulled this way and that. Everyone with his hands out and—"

"This isn't about money," he said curtly. "It's about the welfare of a lot of people. Your decision to become a doctor had something to do with your dedication to the public interest, I assume."

"I don't think my dedication is the issue here," she said evenly. "Don't you understand? I'm too stunned to even comprehend what all this means. I need time, information and the insight to make some decisions. I really don't know what you expect from me."

"You will, if you'll give me a chance to explain. Please, Carolyn. Just hear me out. Then I'll give you the time you need to come to terms with what I'm asking."

His gray eyes were like grappling hooks locking her gaze with his. An undefined warning stirred deep within her. She wanted to turn away, but couldn't. Whether she wanted to or not, she was going to have to deal with this.

She moistened her lips. "All right. But not here in the car. We can talk better inside."

He nodded, and quickly got out and came around

the car to open her door. Without talking, they walked around the house to the outside staircase that led to her apartment. She could feel his warm breath on her neck as she secured her key in the lock and opened the door.

The tiny kitchen was a mess. She'd slept in late and barely made it to her ten o'clock appointment with Bancroft. The tiny living room wasn't much better, and Carolyn wished she'd shut the bedroom door so he couldn't see the discarded clothes on her bed. She'd tried on several outfits before deciding on the summer skirt and blouse.

She swallowed back any apologies or explanation. The apartment was sparsely furnished with the landlady's cast-off furniture. Most of it would have gone begging at a garage sale. An old, scarred desk was loaded down with medical books, papers and a small computer.

In an effort to add some color and personal touches, Carolyn had hung some framed calendar prints and bought a small plant stand. She rarely had any kind of company, and the place looked exactly what it was—rented space.

She avoided looking at Adam as he sat down on the lumpy couch and she took a nearby faded chair. What was he thinking? Why had he intruded on her privacy like this? She was suddenly aware of his masculine presence and the way it filled up the room. He'd left his summer sports jacket in the car and had loosened the matching tie. His short dark hair set off his black eyebrows and arresting gray eyes. His well-built, six-foot frame revealed strong shoulder and arm muscles, and as he casually settled himself into a comfortable position, she resented that he was sending her thoughts into places where she'd placed permanent Keep Out signs.

Her tone was brisker than she'd intended when she said, "All right, I'm listening. Why don't you tell me what this is all about?"

A flicker of expressions like shadows played across his face as he studied her without answering. Then, to her surprise, instead of speaking, he rose abruptly to his feet and walked over to the window. The way he stood there, staring out, she realized that he was experiencing some kind of emotional turmoil of his own. She'd seen patients caught in that same kind of mental maze, and she remained silent, waiting for him to respond.

He stood there for what seemed like an eternity before he turned around and repeated, "What is this all about?"

He walked back to the couch and sat down again. "This is about Marietta."

"Marietta?" Carolyn echoed.

"My late wife. I lost her. She suffered a cruel and painful death."

During her internship at the hospital, she'd seen grief of many kinds. Some people wore the loss of a loved one on the outside, like a mourning cloak, while others held their grief inside, deep and private. It was clear to her that this man's filled the very breath and soul of his being. Until that moment she hadn't really connected with him, but now she saw him from a different perspective, and she felt drawn to him on a level she didn't understand.

"I'm so very sorry," she said, and moved over to the couch beside him.

He searched her face as if to judge the sincerity

of her words as he began to talk about himself. "After I graduated from law school, I took a position as judicial attaché at the United States Embassy in Brazil. I coordinated evidence and information on illegal-substance traffic between the U.S. and Brazil." He paused. "Marietta worked as a translator at the embassy. We'd only been married a few months when she suffered an infection and died from liver failure after a doctor unknowingly gave her an unapproved drug that had found its way into the country through the black market." Carolyn saw the hard set of his jaw and the way his gray eyes glittered like honed steel. "That pharmaceutical drug came from Horizon."

Her stomach took a sickening plunge. "How can you be sure?"

"Drugs are produced in batches," he explained. "Each bottle has the batch number on it, along with the name of the company that manufactured it. The bottle of bad pills that killed Marietta came from Horizon Pharmaceuticals, but when the FDA tried to verify it, the company records showed that a batch with that number had never been produced by the company."

"Then the drug your wife took was a counterfeit," Carolyn said, frowning.

"That's what the authorities believed. I came back to the U.S. a few months ago and found the investigation at a standstill. It's true that illegal organizations that produce counterfeit drugs do their best to duplicate the appearance of the drug by using bottles of the same size, shape and the same kind of labeling."

"So Horizon is telling the truth?"

''I don't think so, and this is why. It's almost impossible to produce an exact match in every detail to an authentic bottle of pills. The size of the lettering may be wrong, the color of the label slightly off, the plastic bottle lighter or heavier, the pills flatter or more rounded. But in this instance, everything in the bottle of pills that killed Marietta is an exact duplicate to one produced by Horizon.''

''How could that be if the company has no record?''

''For the past year products from Horizon have shown up illegally on various foreign black markets, and until now there hasn't been a way for me to penetrate company operations and conduct an on-the-spot investigation.''

Until now. The way he was looking at her left no doubt in her mind what those words meant. She stiffened. He was here with an agenda of his own, and his next words verified it.

''You can provide me with a legitimate cover for my investigation. If I can get in a position to examine the workings of the company from the inside, I'm confident I can find out how black-market drugs that don't meet FDA standards are being illegally circulated in other countries.'' He reached over and took her hand. ''That's why I need your help. You can provide me with a legitimate cover for my investigation.''

''How can I do that?'' she protested. ''I'm totally inexperienced, and it will take time for me to make any changes. You would stick out like a sore thumb if I tried right off to put you in any kind of position at Horizon.''

''I know. That's why we'd have to arrange something different. I'll need a cover that will give me intimate access to the workings of the company.''

The steadiness of his gaze told Carolyn that he had already decided what that cover should be. She felt a strange quiver in her stomach, like someone about to take a plunge off a cliff with a bungee cord tied around her ankle.

''When you arrive at Horizon for the first time, Carolyn, I need to be there with you—as your husband.''

She choked on her intake of breath. ''My husband?''

''In name only,'' he hastened to reassure her. ''Don't you see? It's the perfect cover!''

Chapter Two

"You want to pretend to be my husband?" Her incredulous tone was a mixture of amusement and indignation.

"Well, not pretend, exactly."

"Then what exactly?" Her eyes narrowed and she stiffened beside him.

Adam sensed her instant withdrawal and silently cursed. Damn! He'd come at this the wrong way. What to do now?

He stood up, took a few aimless steps and then eased down on a corner of the old desk. He hoped he could handle the situation better if he wasn't close enough to be aware of every breath she drew. Aware of her soft, womanly warmth. Now, he had to lay all his cards out on the table, and fast. Above all, he had to be honest with her. She wasn't about to jump into anything with her eyes closed.

"It wouldn't all be pretend," he explained, not wanting to hold anything back. "I mean, we'd have to perform all the legalities and officially be husband and wife in case anyone decided to check for a marriage license."

"We would go through a wedding ceremony and

be legally married.'' She tried to keep her voice even. ''Is that what you're saying?''

''Yes, but between us, Carolyn, it would be strictly a business arrangement that would be dissolved once the investigation was over. I'd be a husband to you in name only.''

''A business arrangement? A husband in name only? And how would that work, exactly?'' She raised a questioning eyebrow.

''Well, in public we would have to behave like a congenial couple and—''

''Like newlyweds, perhaps?''

He couldn't help but chuckle. Leave it to her to put her finger exactly where the charade would demand more than she was willing to give. ''We'd be playing a part, acting, pure and simple.''

''A few kisses and hugs between business partners wouldn't mean anything. Is that the way it would work?''

''Exactly. It would be just for show,'' he answered firmly, but as his gaze settled on her pink, kissable lips and the delicate curve of her cheek, he knew he'd have to keep his guard up every moment or he'd blow the whole charade. Everything about her luscious body invited a man's touch. He felt a quiver of desire just thinking about holding her close and kissing her. He'd have to be damn careful not to let her know that he found her utterly sexy and desirable.

''And living arrangements?'' she asked as if reading his thoughts. ''I assume they would demand a little more playacting?''

''The Stanford mansion is large enough for us to have extreme privacy. We could have one wing of the house to ourselves. We would only have to interact with the others when we want their company." He didn't add that an important part of his investigation would involve getting close to Jasper and Della because of their positions in Horizon.

"You have this all figured out, haven't you."

"That's my job. And I'm good at it," he added without conceit. He already had an impressive record, working in Brazil and in the U.S.

"And how long do you anticipate this 'business arrangement' might last?"

"Hopefully just a matter of weeks. Once I have access to company files, I should be able to get the evidence I need to track the illegal shipments." He paused. "There is one other thing, though." He hesitated as if searching for the right words. "There could be complications if all this leads into a murder investigation of your grandfather's death."

"Murder investigation?"

"I told you that the hit-and-run was suspicious." When he saw her lovely face whiten, he cursed himself for being so callous. That was one of the fallouts of being an investigator. You got hardened to things that made a normal person wince.

Her mouth trembled slightly as she asked, "You think the black-market drugs and his hit-and-run might be connected?"

"I don't know, but I promise you I'll do my best to find out." He sat down beside her again. "Look, I feel like a heel pushing you like this, but if we're going to set up this cover, it has to be now, before you move into your role as Carolyn Leigh Stanford. When you meet your uncle and the others living in the Stanford mansion, I'll need to be there as your husband—a fait accompli, so to speak.''

''My…my uncle.'' She stumbled over the term as if it had never crossed her lips before. ''Do you know him?''

From the way her blue eyes widened, he realized that once again he was moving too fast for her. The idea of having a living relative must be as astounding as the rest of this situation.

''I've never met him,'' Adam admitted, ''but I know that Jasper Stanford is a man in his early fifties who's lived with your grandfather for years. He's a laboratory scientist at Horizon and has never shown any aptitude for the business side of the company. As I said before, he was a failure in his own ventures. Jasper was your mother's only sibling. He was twenty-six years old and away at college when she ran away from home at sixteen. Their mother, your grandmother, died a few years after your mother, Alicia, leaving your grandfather a widower for many years.''

Adam paused, trying to decide the best way to explain the situation Carolyn was going to find under her grandfather's roof and at the company. ''Jasper's girlfriend, Della, has been living in the Stanford mansion with her twenty-three-year-old daughter, Lisa, and her twenty-one-year-old son, Buddy. Apparently it was an arrangement that had your grandfather's approval.''

What if I don't like these people? Carolyn asked herself anxiously. And what if they didn't like her? She felt her stomach tighten. She had plenty of memories where she was less than welcome, her presence tolerated only because of the money her foster parents were paid. The circumstances were different now, but one thing was the same. These people were going to resent her presence big-time.

"Were they mentioned in my grandfather's will?"

"You and Jasper are the major beneficiaries. I'm sure that the contents of your grandfather's will was totally unexpected, though, and your inheritance a great surprise to all of them."

Was there a warning in his tone? She shivered. Too much was coming at her too fast. She needed a break. Quickly she rose to her feet.

"I missed my second cup of coffee at breakfast," she said. "Would you care for a cup?"

The invitation wasn't exactly full of warmth and hospitality, but he readily accepted and then followed her into the small kitchen. She motioned to one of the chairs at the chipped Formica table crowded into one corner.

"Cream and sugar?" she asked as she took a couple of mugs down from the cupboard.

"No, black."

"Good, because I don't have any cream," she admitted with a wry smile. "Going grocery shopping is not one of my things."

"Not mine, either. I knew we had something in common," he added facetiously, hoping for a smile, but as she handed him the mug, her expression was anything but amused.

Instead of sitting down in the other chair, she leaned against the kitchen counter, sipping her own coffee. Even though they were in close physical proximity, she seemed able to completely disregard him. Everything in her body language told him she was processing what he had told her. He wouldn't have been surprised if she'd taken her mug and disappeared into the other room, ignoring him completely.

He'd bungled everything. He'd completely misjudged Carolyn Leigh. The instant she'd locked those clear, ocean blue eyes on him, he should have known her outward feminine softness was deceiving. She had a self-reliance that was a match for his or anyone else's. Arthur Stanford must have been aware of her strength and firm hold on her convictions when he decided to leave his assets to her. He doubted very much that she'd ever be swayed by pure emotion or easily dominated by a husband, pretend or otherwise. If she agreed to his plan, she'd be a tremendous help, but if she refused to consider a contrived marriage, there would be nothing he could do or say to make her change her mind.

He forced himself to remain silent, sipping his coffee. His wandering gaze settled on a kitchen shelf that held a small vase of artificial flowers, a chipped porcelain tea cup, and a small framed photo of an older woman standing with a frail-looking blond girl who appeared to be about eight. Carolyn? It must be.

"Yes, it's me." She startled him by suddenly sitting down in the other chair and following his gaze to the photo.

"And who's the woman?" he asked.

"An angel." A soft glow deepened the blue of her eyes. "Hannah Lamm. When I was a sickly, emaciated three-year-old, who had no appeal as a child to be adopted, she arranged to take me into her home. She nurtured me through all the childhood diseases. I stayed with her until I was eight. She saved my life. My physical health improved, and so did my mental abilities. Hannah convinced me that I had a good mind and could learn. Somehow she planted the idea that I could become a doctor. When she died and I was thrown back into the pack of unwanted orphans, when I thought life wasn't worth living, that goal was the motivation that kept me going.''

''And you've supported yourself all the way?''

She nodded. ''Hannah also taught me that goals are reached by working for them. I got a full-time job out of high school and was lucky enough to get with a good company and the chance to learn a lot about investments. Even after I started college, I worked part-time. Sometimes I was tempted to stay with Champion Realty and Investments, because I could see myself moving up in the company, but somehow I had to prove to myself—and to Hannah—that I could have an M.D. after my name.''

''And now you do. Congratulations. You have a medical degree and more. Your grandfather had great faith in you, Carolyn, and he must have loved your mother very much to leave almost everything he had to her daughter.''

''All this is too sudden. I still can't believe it.'' Her fingers tightened on her cup. ''How could my life change so radically in the span of a few moments?''

''That's the way it does sometimes, both good and bad. But nothing stays the same, and we really don't have much choice how to handle change. We can make it work for us or just mark time.''

The challenge in his tone was clear, but she ignored it. She wasn't ready to make any kind of a commitment. Certainly not the kind he was proposing. She needed time. Time! She glanced at the kitchen clock. Almost one o'clock. She was due at the free clinic at twelve-thirty.

"What's the matter?" he asked as panic flashed across her face.

"It's my afternoon at Friends Free Clinic." She hurriedly got to her feet. "I completely forgot. Oh, no. My car. Taking a bus will eat up another hour."

"Well, if mine is still working, I think we're in business."

She nodded. "Thank you. I'm surprised Dr. Mc-Pherson hasn't called to chew me out. He's an ornery old codger who should have retired years ago, but he can't ignore the need. Just a minute while I grab my medical bag."

"What about lunch?" he asked as if he hadn't been planning on coaxing her to have it with him.

"I'm used to skipping it."

"Doctor, doctor," he teased. "For shame."

She laughed then, a full, wonderful laugh that wrinkled her nose, brought a shine to her crystalline blue eyes. She was utterly beautiful. Vibrant. And desirable. He was stunned by the sudden realization that Carolyn Leigh was about to touch some guarded depth of emotion that he thought he'd put away forever. He couldn't afford such feelings. First of all, she was on the threshold of a lifestyle of money and prestige, and getting involved with her would go nowhere. Second, any personal feelings would wreak havoc with the impersonal marriage of convenience that was vital to the success of his mission.

It would be pure idiocy to allow himself to be attracted to her on any level.

Carolyn directed him to the clinic, which was housed in an old building that had once been a small neighborhood school. The place was still run-down and in need of remodeling, but the first floor had been refurbished to handle the various demands of a free clinic.

A valiant sun had lost its battle to the overcast sky and a soft rain began to fall as he let her out of the car.

"Thanks a bunch," Carolyn said quickly as she prepared to make a dash for the front door.

"Carolyn, will you think about what I've said?"

"I'll...I'll be in touch."

From the look on his face, Carolyn knew he was expecting more than this vague promise, but at the moment it was all she had to give. If he'd pushed her for an answer to his proposition, it would have been an immediate and definite No!

"I could give you a ride home," he suggested.

"Thanks, but I'll catch a ride with someone from the clinic when it closes."

As she hurried away, she could feel his intense gaze on her back. Why in the world hadn't she told him straight out that playing house with him was out of the question? She sympathized with his personal loss, admired his dedication to his job, but she wasn't cut out for a game of deception. Just pretending to be his wife, and opening herself up to all kinds of undefined emotions, was more than she could handle.

"Well, now. Who's the hunk that made you late?" Rosie DiPaloa teased as Carolyn hurried into the reception area. Obviously the dark-haired young woman had been looking out the window as Adam drove up in front of the building. "Don't tell me our brand-new doctor is spreading her wings already. What gives?"

"Sorry to disappoint you, Rosie. Nothing gives. I'm late because of a business meeting. And my car won't start—again. Would you have your brother pull it into his garage?"

"Sure," Rosie said, and wrote down the address Carolyn gave her. "That car's spending more time in Tony's garage than it is on the streets. Why don't you let Tony look for a nice clean, used car for you? Trade up to something that'll keep running for a while? You ought to be able to afford it now."

For a second Carolyn thought Rosie was referring to her inheritance. Then she realized her friend meant that Carolyn would be going into practice somewhere soon. How would Rosie respond if she knew that very soon Carolyn would be able to buy the latest, most expensive car on the road? Or if Carolyn told her she'd be moving out of her small apartment to live in a mansion? A sickening feeling accompanied Carolyn's sudden realization that she would probably lose Rosie's friendship and that of her bulging Italian family once her inheritance became known. Her lack of money and indebtedness had been something she had in common with them. They had opened their hearts to her because she was one of them, but her grandfather's will would change all that.

"What's the matter?" Rosie asked with her usual bluntness. "Are you sure you don't have something to tell me?"

"Not now," Carolyn answered firmly. There would be time later to sort all of it out. At the moment she was a doctor with patients waiting. She grabbed her white coat, slung her stethoscope around her neck and said, "Give me five minutes and then start sending them in."

WHEN ADAM PULLED INTO Bancroft's parking lot, he saw that Carolyn's car was gone.

"A tow truck took it away," the lawyer's receptionist told him. "I think the sign said DiPaloa Brothers Garage. Is there a problem?"

"No, I was just curious."

Mr. Bancroft poked his head out of his office. "I thought I heard your voice, Adam. Come in. I saw you drive away with Dr. Leigh. Bring me up-to-date."

"There's not much to update," he confessed as he dropped into one of the leather office chairs. "I spent a couple of hours with her. She listened, asked a few questions and said she'd be in touch."

"Do you think she'll come around once the shock of all this wears off a little?"

"Damn, I don't know what to think. We both know she could be in danger the minute she steps inside Horizon Pharmaceuticals. Carolyn is as sharp as they come, and it's a given that she won't be played for any kind of patsy. One way or another, she'll educate herself about the business, and without realizing it, she may bring to light something that will force a killer into action."

"Do you think that's what happened to her grandfather?" asked the lawyer.

"I'm convinced of it." Adam ran agitated fingers

through his hair. "Someone is determined to use Horizon for the shipment of black-market drugs, and Carolyn could be an innocent victim of their treachery if she gets too close to the truth."

"Well, you'll have a better chance to protect her if you're on the scene as her husband. Didn't you explain that to her?"

"I didn't want to scare her into agreeing to my plan, but I gave her enough background for her to realize that this isn't just a parlor game someone is playing. I'm not sure she's convinced that Horizon is involved. I wish I had more concrete evidence to support the theory that someone in the company is raking in big bucks by diverting these drugs overseas." He sighed. "For some reason, I was hoping to appeal to a deeper commitment to see justice done."

"That's a lot to expect from a young woman whose been treated as disposable by almost everyone in her life. You have to admire her for her accomplishments."

"I do. Very much." He felt admiration and a great deal more, he silently admitted. Carolyn Leigh had touched him on more levels than he thought possible. An unbidden sweet heat curled deep within him when he looked at her, and it had been a long time since he'd wanted to touch a woman, to feel her skin beneath his fingertips and lips. He shifted uncomfortably in the leather chair as if Bancroft might be able to read his lustful thoughts.

"What are you going to do now?"

"I'm trying to make up my mind. It's a delicate balance, trying to put pressure on her, or backing off and hoping that she'll come around before it's too late." Adam's jaw tightened. "One thing's for sure. Come hell or high water, I hope I'm with her when she innocently steps into a situation that has all the earmarks of internal combustion."

CAROLYN GLANCED AT the clock. Five-fifteen. The clinic closed at six, so she had time for one more patient. She signaled for Rosie to send someone into her examination room.

"Hello," she said, smiling at the young Mexican couple with a baby who'd entered the examining room. The father spoke halting English.

"You make José well?" he asked anxiously. They were itinerant farm workers and their six-month-old baby had taken ill with a cough and fever. The mother looked no older than seventeen.

Carolyn quickly examined the infant and determined that his illness was due to strep throat, which could be controlled with antibiotics. The medication needed to be taken for two weeks. Since it was expensive, Carolyn checked their supply of sample medications. She plucked three small bottles from the shelf, an amount that would cover the two-week period.

As she held them in her hand, ready to give to the anxious parents, she glanced at the label. Horizon Pharmaceuticals.

Her hand tightened on the bottles. Since the rest of the samples had been safely given out, Carolyn rationalized that they must have contained genuine safe antibiotics.

But what if they weren't *safe?* Adam's compelling voice echoed in her ears. Her mouth went dry, and for a long moment she just stood there staring at the bottles in her hand. In her mind's eye she saw herself handing over medication that was faulty—and could kill.

"Miss Doctor, something is matter?" asked the young man, worried by Carolyn's sudden stillness.

"No, nothing," she quickly assured him. She disposed of the bottles in her hand and handed him three that had come from a different supplier. She spoke slowly and carefully, making sure he understood when to give the medication to the baby.

"Bless you, bless you," the mother kept saying as Carolyn walked them out to the waiting room with them.

Rosie quickly locked the door after them. "Whew, what a day. Dr. McPherson took off early and left me with a mound of paperwork." She eyed Carolyn's preoccupied look with suspicion. "You look miles away. If I didn't know better, I'd think you had a man on your mind."

"How did you know?" Carolyn took a deep breath and gave Rosie a tentative smile. "I'm thinking about getting married."

Chapter Three

Adam stood up as Carolyn and a dark-haired young woman came out of the clinic. He'd been sitting on one of the benches on the small porch outside the front door. According to a posted sign, the clinic closed at six. It was a few minutes past, and he was wondering what to do if she didn't appear soon.

When she saw him, a startled expression crossed her face. He gave her a warm smile in the hope of defusing some of her expected indignation.

"I wanted to make sure you had a way home," he said quickly. "Your car was gone from the parking lot, and I didn't know whether it was running or not."

He tried to read her reaction as she walked slowly toward him, and steeled himself for a brisk rebuttal or an ice-cold glare. What he never expected in a million years was for her to give him a bright, welcoming smile.

As she moved to his side, she said, "How sweet of you, darling."

When she slipped a possessive arm through his, Adam had trouble masking his astonishment. Was this the same woman he dropped off only a few hours ago?

"I was just talking about you and our whirlwind courtship," Carolyn continued, still smiling. "Rosie, meet Adam Lawrence, my fiancé."

Rosie gave him a frank, measuring look. "I can't believe this."

Neither can I, Adam admitted silently, thankful for the experience he'd had in shifting his perspective on a second's notice. Smiling pleasantly, he said, "Nice to meet you, Rosie."

"Likewise, but I tell you, this is a doozy of a surprise. Imagine Carolyn keeping something like this a secret! I've been telling her she should be looking around for someone to keep her tootsies warm at night, but every time I tried to line up some available guy, she'd give me that 'Cool it, Rosie,' look. Now I know why. Are you from around here, Adam?" she asked, and added pointedly, "What do you do?"

Adam sensed Carolyn stiffen. Her muscles tensed as if she was going to try to answer. Before she could, Adam said smoothly, "Well, it's kind of hard to explain what I do, Rosie. I guess you could say my title is corporation efficiency expert. What that means is various companies hire me to take a look at their operations and see how I can streamline them. That's why I'm in Seattle, cleaning up the various corporate businesses in this area."

As he talked, he squeezed Carolyn's arm reassuringly. Undoubtedly, she was as surprised as Rosie to hear the lies rolling off his tongue. Fortunately the agency had set up this cover before he left Washington. The false identity would provide a reasonable excuse for examining the inner workings of Horizon if Carolyn's cooperation provided him with the entrance he needed.

"He's originally from New Mexico," Carolyn volunteered, beginning to play her part with an ease that totally surprised her.

"Really? A lot of my family are from that part of the country. There are DiPaloas all over the Southwest. Maybe you've run into some of them."

"We'll have to compare notes sometime," Adam answered smoothly.

"Carolyn, I thought your life was nothing but study, study, work and more work. You never once hinted there was a handsome Romeo in the picture."

"I was waiting until after graduation to tell you. That's why I'm not wearing a ring. But now, we're ready to tell everyone, aren't we, darling?"

"Yes, it's time everyone knew," he concurred readily. The glint in her eye told him she was enjoying challenging him to carry out the deception exactly as he'd proposed. "I've got a nice evening planned for us, sweetheart. Kind of a private celebration. Dinner, maybe dancing, and then..." He let his voice trail off suggestively.

"Sounds lovely," she murmured, but he could see the color rise in her cheeks, and she squeezed his arm as if she wished it was his neck.

"Wait'll I get home and tell the family you're getting married, Carolyn. You'll have to bring Adam over for closer inspection. I know there'll be a lot of questions about the wedding and everything. You'll make a beautiful bride." She beamed at Carolyn, her eyes suddenly misty.

"Yes, she will," Adam said quickly, afraid that

if Rosie started asking about their wedding plans, Carolyn would blurt out the truth. He didn't know what had happened to make her agree to the pretense, but he suspected from her sudden rigidity that she was having second thoughts. The talk about a wedding had brought up some issues she was not ready to handle.

"We're going to be pretty busy, I'm afraid," Adam said quickly and as smoothly as he could.

"I don't suppose you'll be continuing here at the clinic, Carolyn." Rosie sighed. "Dr. McPherson isn't going to be happy."

"I'll try to find someone to take my place," Carolyn promised. Responding to Adam's firm hold on her arm, she said something vague about calling later. As they walked away, she felt Rosie's measuring glance on them and wondered if her friend had bought the preposterous lie.

The early-evening sky was clearing and the air was brisk and fresh as they climbed into his car. Adam didn't turn on the ignition immediately. He couldn't tell from the way Carolyn's jaw was clenched whether she was angry or just about to cry.

"I can't do it," she said in a strained voice. Her lower lip quivered, and he could see that her hands were clasped tightly together on her lap. "I wanted to, but I can't."

He couldn't imagine what had happened to cause her to look so tortured, so filled with anguish. He wanted to put his arm around her, draw her close and ease that anguish, but suppressed the impulse. This was no time to offer anything until he found out where she was coming from. The way he handled the next few moments might well determine her decision to play out the deception or stop it before it had gone any further.

He turned in the seat, gave her all his attention and waited for her to go on. When she remained silent, he asked gently, "What happened, Carolyn?"

She didn't look at him, but he could see the struggle going on within her. The rapid rise and fall of her chest was proof that she was fighting some deep emotion. He was relieved when she finally turned to him. She kept her hands tightly clasped in her lap as she told him about the young Mexican couple and their sick baby.

"I explained that the baby had strep throat that could be healed with antibiotics. When I was about to offer them a bottle of pills with the Horizon label, the horror of black-market drugs suddenly became real. I felt a stab of fear. What if the bottles I held in my hand had come from some illegal source? What if the pills were contaminated?" She raised pain-stricken eyes to his. "What if the parents gave them to their baby in good faith?"

"The baby might die," he answered evenly.

"And it would be my fault."

"Not if you didn't know they were contaminated. A lot of innocent people are buying and dispensing these drugs. It is the suppliers who are guilty. They deliberately put these unapproved drugs on the market. The only place to stop them is at the source, Carolyn."

"Like Horizon Pharmaceuticals," she echoed in a strained voice.

"Yes, which is what my investigation is all about. And that's why I've come to you for help."

Her lip trembled "I want to turn my back on all

of this, but how can I live with myself if I don't do what you ask?''

"That's a question I can't answer."

She sighed. "When I looked at that baby, saw the trust the young couple had in me, I guess I knew the answer. I didn't have a choice, not if I wanted to live with my conscience." Her head came up. "And that's why I lied to Rosie."

He reached over and took her hand. "You made the right decision. I promise you you'll never regret it." He silently prayed that he could keep her on the edge of his investigation and out of danger.

She swallowed hard. "But I don't know if I can do it. Lies. Lies. Rosie's my only friend. She's excited about my having found someone to marry. It's all such a sham! I hate being deceitful."

"I don't like it, either, and I've tried to figure out other ways to conduct the investigation but came up empty. Unless I can get on the inside of Horizon, this horrible traffic will continue." His eyes hardened. "And God only knows how many more will die." *Like Marietta.*

A weighted silence stretched between them until she mentally shook herself and asked, "All right. What happens next?"

He searched her face for a long minute, then smiled and said, "Dinner."

They drove to a small restaurant that overlooked Lake Washington. Carolyn had never been there before, and she was relieved to see that it was a low-key, family-owned establishment that offered a modest menu.

"I found it when I was looking for a home-cooked meal," Adam volunteered when they were seated by a window with brightly colored café curtains.

Even though Carolyn had missed lunch, she had little appetite. She ordered a seafood salad, while Adam opted for roast beef, mashed potatoes and peas. As she sipped a glass of white wine, she was grateful that his easy conversation didn't demand any forced participation. He seemed to know that small talk was all she could handle while she collected her thoughts. It wasn't until she was nearly finished with her salad that she felt like asking some nagging questions.

"Is it really true that you're from New Mexico?"

"Of course it's true. Would I lie?" he asked in mock indignation.

"Only with every other breath," she said, returning his teasing smile. "All that stuff about you being an efficiency expert. You expect people to believe that?"

"It's the best cover we could come up with. I needed an identity that would allow me to examine everything inherent in Horizon's production and sale of pharmaceutical drugs. I think the cover will work. With your cooperation, of course."

"You're sure about this?"

"I'd be lying if I promised you a hundred-percent guarantee of success. There are myriad ways that the whole thing could fall apart. That's why both of us will have to watch our steps carefully."

She tensed. "I've never been very good at make-believe. What if I foul up?"

"We have to make certain that doesn't happen. You did very well tonight with Rosie." He smiled reassuringly. "If you can fool your closest friend, you shouldn't have any trouble with a bunch of strangers.''

''I'm going to be dumped into the lives of people who have every reason to hate my guts. You can bet that there won't be any welcome mat put out for me. I have no idea how I should behave in such a high-class environment. I've never known any people with money, never even visited anyone who lives in a mansion.''

''That's all right,'' he replied quickly. ''Maybe you'll do something that doesn't quite fit, but people will expect you to make mistakes. And that's good, because it will disarm them.''

''So the dumber I look and act, the better?'' Her tone was slightly caustic.

''I didn't mean that at all,'' he said with a chuckle. ''I just meant that you will be faced with some unexpected challenges, and I want you to be careful, that's all.''

''Careful not to make a fool of myself? I can't promise anything in that regard.'' Carolyn had had some unpleasant experiences at the hospital with people who tried to throw their weight and wealth around when the rules and procedures didn't suit them. ''I have no idea how to relate to rich people,'' she admitted.

''You'll learn. Their focus in life is fashioned by tradition and the affluent world in which they live. They have hidden agendas and structure their behavior according to what's deemed acceptable in their social stratum.''

''You know all this because…?'' As the lines on his forehead deepened, she had her answer. ''You come from money, don't you.''

"Not anymore. My father was a New York stock-broker," Adam told her. "I was an only child and had every advantage when I was growing up—prep school, college, the whole works. My senior year, the market dropped out from under my father's investments, and he lost almost everything. His heart couldn't take the strain, and when he died, my mother was left with a small income. She moved to New Mexico to live. When I came back from Brazil, I spent some time with her." He gave Carolyn a rueful smile. "So you see, I was almost telling the truth when I said I was from there."

She should have known. Everything about him suggested a privileged upbringing. His polished manner and easy confidence. His suit had obviously been tailored to fit. His fingernails appeared nicely cared for, and the cut of his dark hair accented his strong, masculine features. He could enter any elite social gathering and blend in without effort. How could she even make a pretense of being his wife?

She lowered her eyes as she imagined him in a tuxedo, perfectly groomed at a country club party, or lounging beside a fashionable swimming pool, a martini in his hand. The vision of him in only swimming trunks stirred an unbidden warmth—one that caused an instant denial to shoot through her. She couldn't be attracted to him on that level. There absolutely couldn't be anything sexual between them. He'd made it clear that he was only interested in her as a means to conduct his investigation. She'd be a fool if she allowed herself to make anything more of it than that.

"I'm not sure I'm up to playing out this charade," she said defensively. Not only were her own emotions getting in the way, but the likelihood of her causing him embarrassment seemed too great. She had an unpleasant childhood memory of the time some rich woman had invited a bunch of orphans to her house for a party. Carolyn had been so nervous she'd turned the whole plate of ice cream and cake over in her lap. Even now, she shuddered at the recollection. Just making the lifestyle transition she faced would be difficult enough, but having him privy to every word and mishap made it even worse.

"I want to make this as easy on you as possible, Carolyn. I'll do my best to arrange things so you don't feel threatened in any way. I promise to make no demands that aren't vital to the success of my investigation." He paused. "Do you understand what I'm saying?"

She knew then that he was aware of the attraction that had flared between them. She nodded. "All of this is just part of a business arrangement. Nothing more." She realized she was addressing herself as much as him.

"Right. As for getting married, there's no need for anything but a civil service, one we'll have as quickly and quietly as possible. We can dispense with everything else."

Everything else? All the dreams? All expectations of someday being a bride in white lace and satin? To love and to cherish? She had always thought that someday she'd hear those poignant words, and she'd never feel lonely again. Getting married would be a beginning of a new life and the ending of an old one.

"All we need are the official credentials of Mr.

and Mrs. Adam Lawrence," he assured her. "And you'll need to go by Carolyn Lawrence until this is over. For your protection, Mr. Bancroft will go over any legal matters that might come up while the investigation is going on."

Investigation, he had said, not marriage. Just a business arrangement. Of course, that was all it was. No reason for her to get sentimental about taking vows that meant nothing. In a way that was what her life had been up till now. Pragmatic. Realistic. No reason for her to view a wedding ring on her finger as anything but a cold circle of metal.

"How soon should we do this?" she asked, putting her hands in her lap and clasping them tightly.

"Bancroft will make arrangements for you to move into the house and will finalize all the business arrangements. Just a matter of a few days, I think."

"So soon?" She forced a light laugh. "You really know how to rush a girl off her feet."

"The sooner we get into position, the better."

Get into position. That's the way he was viewing this whole marriage arrangement. Professional. Unemotional. Nonpersonal. The moment had come when she was either going to believe him or walk away.

"I'll check my wardrobe and see if I have something decent to wear to a pretend wedding."

They went back to making idle conversation, and as soon as they'd finished their coffee and apple cobbler, they left the restaurant.

The silence between them on the ride back to her apartment was like a thick curtain as Carolyn's sensible nature began to question everything Adam Lawrence had said. Was this so-called investigation of Horizon just an elaborate scheme to swindle a naive heiress? Bancroft was the only one vouching for Adam Lawrence, and what did she really know about the lawyer? Had she bought into some sophisticated hoax?

"How would I go about verifying everything you've told me?" she asked as Adam walked her up the stairs to her back door. In the dim light of the back-door bulb, she could see his eyes widen in surprise. It was obvious he was taken aback by her question.

"You could decide to initiate a background check on Adam Lawrence."

With sudden insight she said, "That's not even your real name, is it."

"For the moment it's the only legal name I have."

She wanted to laugh, but the mirth caught in her chest. She turned away and went in the house without even responding to his, "Good night. I'll call you in the morning."

BACK IN HIS HOTEL ROOM, Adam called his supervisor, Angelica Rivers, a woman whose crisp, businesslike voice matched her appearance. Adam guessed that at this early hour, she was probably still wearing her tailored white blouse and the straight linen skirt with its matching long jacket. Angelica had been with the agency since she was twenty, and now in her forties, she brooked no nonsense from agents, male or female.

"It's a go," Adam told her.

"Carolyn Leigh agreed?"

"Yes," he answered, and mentally crossed his

fingers that the arrangement with Carolyn was still a go.

"What kind of woman is she?"

Adam knew he had to be careful. Angelica would weigh everything he said and probably read between the lines. "We can trust her. She's ready to cooperate fully."

"I repeat, what kind of woman is she? Are you afraid to offer a personal evaluation, Adam?"

"No, not really," he lied. His personal evaluation of Carolyn Leigh demanded honesty about how attractive he found her—in more aspects than he was willing to admit to his boss.

"You don't like this woman who is going to pretend to be your wife?" Before he could answer, she added with knowing perception, "Or is it, as I suspect, just the opposite?"

"That's what I like about you, Angel," he said, using her nickname. "Nobody can accuse you of holding back. Why don't you just ask me if she turns me on?"

"Well, does she? You know darn well you can't get emotionally involved when you're on a case—especially this one. Maybe I should send someone else in right now. You could get yourself killed if you let things get out of hand."

"I'm not going to let anything get out of hand. That's a promise. And you don't need to worry about Carolyn not sticking to the cover." He told Angelica about the Mexican couple and their baby. "She's a dedicated humanitarian, and she convinced herself that she wanted to cooperate." *Unless she's changed her mind.*

"What's the plan?"

"We'll arrange a civil marriage ceremony as soon as the lawyer has all the legal ends tied up in a few days. Then we'll move into the Stanford mansion and meet some of the players."

"So the curtain goes up."

"Yes." Adam drew in a deep breath, and as confidently as he could, said, "And the drama begins!"

Chapter Four

Carolyn spent the next three days verifying every fact she could about her inheritance, and she satisfied herself that she could trust Mr. Bancroft. The lawyer's personal reputation and that of his firm was without blemish. As promised, he had arranged for a substantial amount of money to be deposited in her bank account and had given her the assurance that it was only a fraction of the assets that would follow. She requested that he draw up a prenuptial agreement to protect her inheritance, and when she expressed her concerns about Adam's plan to use her to expedite his investigation, the lawyer was quick to assure her that it was important for her to know the truth about possible criminal activities at Horizon as soon as possible.

"The suspicions about Horizon need to be proved or laid to rest."

Carolyn decided that his advice was valid, and only five days after her life had been turned upside down, she sat stiffly beside Adam as he drove through the upscale neighborhood where the Stanford mansion was located. As she looked at the million-dollar homes they were passing, Carolyn thought that Alice must have felt like this when she fell down the rabbit hole. Nervously she moistened her lips and smoothed the folds of her pink linen dress.

The marriage ceremony that morning had gone very much as Adam had predicted. Mr. Bancroft had arranged for a friend of his, a justice of the peace, to read the service in the lawyer's office. It only took ten minutes, and they could have been applying for a driver's license for all the emotion that was displayed.

Carolyn viewed the ring that Adam slipped on her finger with a feeling of detachment, and he seemed to receive his with the same indifference. The only time she'd been jerked back to reality was when Bancroft addressed her after the ceremony as Mrs. Lawrence.

"I've alerted Jasper Stanford that all legalities have been taken care of, Mrs. Lawrence," the lawyer explained. "And I've answered all of his questions about the inheritance and your marriage plans. He knows you will be arriving with your husband sometime today. I wish you both well." Then he added with obvious double meaning, "And success."

Adam thanked him as he shook the man's hand. "I appreciate your help."

The ceremony had gone better than Adam had anticipated. He'd been ready to deal with Carolyn's last-minute trepidations, but she had maintained her composure throughout and handled herself beautifully.

He couldn't have found a better woman to play out the dangerous undercover investigation ahead of them. Nor a more attractive one, he thought as she stood beside him, wearing a simple summer dress that hugged her slender lines and curves. He was aware of every breath she drew. Her honey-tinted hair drifted softly on her shoulders, and a simple strand of imitation pearls was her only accessory. She had flatly rejected any flowers, making it clear that they would be out of place in this husband-and-wife impersonation.

Her eyes had widened in surprise when he lightly brushed her lips in the traditional wedding kiss, and he was startled by his own desire to deepen the contact and taste the tantalizing sweetness of her mouth. He felt her stiffen and wondered if his desire had been reflected in his eyes. Great, just great, he thought. It had been a long time since he'd wanted to take a woman in his arms. Such feelings in this situation spelled disaster, and he didn't doubt for a minute that she'd withdraw her cooperation if he moved out of line.

WHEN THEY LEFT THE lawyer's office in Adam's car, an uncomfortable silence fell between them. He gave his attention to his driving, and as Carolyn cast him a sidelong glance, she saw a handsome stranger in a tailored dark suit, white shirt and silk tie. And he was her legal husband. That fact alone was beyond comprehension. As she stared at the beautiful diamond ring on her finger, she kept reminding herself that none of this was for real.

The past few days had been a whirlwind, and her emotions had taken a beating. As her life swiftly moved into a completely foreign dimension, she wasn't certain she could cope with all the demands and changes.

She'd finally gotten up the courage to tell Rosie that she was leaving the clinic and why. They'd been sitting on a park bench, eating hot dogs for lunch, and Rosie just laughed with a dismissive wave of her hand when Carolyn tried to tell her what had happened.

"Sure, somebody died and left you a bundle, sure. And I'm related to the Queen of England. Who are you kidding? You don't have to spin a tale for me if you're about to run off with that handsome hunk. More power to you, I say."

Carolyn took a deep breath. "It's true. I don't even know how much money I've inherited."

Rosie's dark eyes grew wider as Carolyn explained about her grandfather's will and the fact that he'd been financing her college education. When she'd finished, Rosie put down her hot dog and stared at Carolyn as if she expected her to laugh and say, "Gotcha."

Carolyn couldn't blame her friend for expecting a joke. The two of them had spun tales of marrying a rich man someday or winning the lottery, but none of their fantasies had come close to the story Carolyn was telling.

"It's really true, Rosie," Carolyn quietly insisted. "I've arranged for someone to take my place at the clinic." She didn't add that she'd obligated herself to pay the replacement doctor for his services. Adam had warned her not to say anything about their getting married until they'd moved into the mansion. He didn't want anyone involved in the ceremony.

"As soon as I get settled," she'd gone on to her

friend, "you can come and let me show you around."

Carolyn could tell by the way Rosie reacted that their friendship was already threatened. A gulf was starting to widen between them, and Carolyn knew that until Adam's investigation was over, it would be better to try to pretend that everything was romantically "wine and roses" in her marriage. Rosie would be aghast at the truth.

Carolyn returned to the present. There was no doubt in her mind that the Stanford mansion would be as large and intimidating as any of the homes they were passing. What were the people like who lived in them? She took a deep breath and asked Adam point-blank what to expect when they got to the Stanford mansion.

"It's bound to be a little tense and uncomfortable at first," he told her. "We'll just have to take it as it comes." His own thoughts had been following the same kind of speculation, and to be perfectly honest, he didn't know what the situation might be. People were unpredictable at best. He had no idea how Carolyn's uncle was going to receive her, or how the Jasper's live-in significant other would, either. From all accounts, Della Denison had grandfather's approval as an executive at Horizon, and the woman wasn't likely to accept Carolyn's presence in the company with open arms.

Adam was also concerned about the way Lisa and Buddy Denison were going to treat Carolyn. He considered them self-centered and spoiled. They could make life hell for her in a thousand different ways.

"I wish I'd had more time to get ready for this," Carolyn said honestly. But would she ever be ready?

She glanced at the man sitting beside her. What did she really know about him? She couldn't believe that she had put herself in his hands—in more ways than one.

"Just stick to the script we worked out. Don't try to embellish any of the details. Remember, don't supply extra information when you're pushed into a corner. Everyone's going to be curious about you, about us, but you don't have to satisfy their curiosity. You're in the driver's seat in this situation. You have the power and the money."

"Power and money." She wanted to laugh at the irony of it. When on earth had she ever possessed either one of them? A few pieces of paper couldn't change her basic perception of herself.

"The first thing you'll want to do is buy yourself a car, a good one."

"I suppose so. Before I told Rosie about my inheritance, her brother called me and told me to junk my old one. He wanted me to look at a couple of used models he had for sale that were in better shape. I told him I'd think about it."

"That's all?" He raised an eyebrow. "You didn't tell him you were in a position to buy the latest, most expensive model on the road?"

She shook her head. "I wanted Rosie to know first."

He nodded. "I can understand that, but you need to feel free to spend the money that is rightfully yours, Carolyn. I imagine that you'll be needing a whole new wardrobe, won't you?"

Shopping? Whole new wardrobe? She was used to buying only clothes she absolutely needed. Even with her new ample bank account, she had only made a few inexpensive purchases. In fact, the thrift stores had been a common target for Rosie and her when they needed something. She realized that all that was going to change. Expensive trappings and a make-believe marriage would make demands she'd never even dreamed about. That scared her. She'd always been her own person, making her own way, and now she was about to turn that control over to people she didn't even know in order to play a role.

Adam saw the color drain from her lovely face. What was she thinking? Had he been honest enough with her about the situation? If only there was another way not to involve her—but there wasn't. She was the cover he needed. His hands tightened on the wheel.

As they drove through the iron gates of the Stanford mansion, Carolyn gasped in disbelief. A three-story gray-stone mansion rose in palatial grandeur, its setting one of velvet green lawns and beautifully landscaped gardens. She could see a five-car garage, a greenhouse and beyond these structures, a modern boathouse hugging one of the numerous waterways around Seattle. Her mind utterly refused to accept that a few signed papers had made all of this hers. This had to be a mistake. A monstrous mistake.

Adam stopped the car in front of a line of long, shallow steps framed by marble pillars. Two wings of the mansion spread on either side of a pair of carved doors, flanked by tall, beveled-glass windows.

As they sat there looking at the structure, the shadow of the huge house engulfed the car. Neither

Carolyn nor Adam moved for a long moment. Then Adam asked quietly, "Are you ready?"

The question hung in the air between them. As if the moment of truth had come, Carolyn drew a steadying breath. "Yes, I'm ready."

"Good." He smiled at her. "Let's do it then."

After helping her from the car, he set his matched traveling suitcases on the sidewalk beside her single bag. "Someone will bring them in."

She nodded, as if she wasn't used to toting her own bags everywhere she went. Even when she'd attended a couple of medical conferences, she'd always avoided the eyes of bellhops as she carried her own suitcase. The memory brought a hint of a smile.

Adam put a guiding hand on her arm as they climbed the steps. He rang the doorbell, and as she stood nervously at his side, he winked at her. "Would you like to have me carry you across the threshold for show?"

"It might make a grand entrance," she agreed with false levity, and they were both smiling when the door open.

A tall, angular woman in a housekeeper's uniform stood there, glaring at them. Carolyn would have taken a step backward and apologized for the interruption, but Adam just nodded and said, "Mr. and Mrs. Lawrence. We're expected."

"There's no one at home at present," the woman informed them tartly.

"I see," Adam replied as he guided Carolyn past the housekeeper and into the house. "And your name is?"

"Morna. I've been housekeeper for Arthur Stanford for nigh on twenty years." Her eyes centered on Carolyn as her mouth tightened. "And my husband, Mack, he's the groundskeeper."

"I'm sure my grandfather was very fortunate to have you in his service," Carolyn heard herself saying, as if accustomed to handling servants who obviously disliked her on sight.

"Do you know when Mr. Stanford is expected home?" Adam asked.

"He and Ms. Denison are out for the day," Morna answered crisply. "I understand that you are to occupy the master suite, is that correct?"

Carolyn nodded as if this had been previously arranged. She could tell from the housekeeper's turned-down mouth that the arrangement did not sit well with her.

"This way. Mack will bring your luggage." She gave a pointed glance at the unimpressive suitcases and then led the way across the wide marble foyer to a staircase that curved up and out of sight.

As they climbed the steps to the second floor, Carolyn's eyes were drawn to a series of impressive portraits hanging on the wall. Were these her ancestors? Which one of the staid gentlemen was her grandfather? Could the older woman with white hair be her grandmother? Carolyn's heartbeat quickened. Was there a portrait of her mother hanging somewhere in the house?

Adam could tell that Carolyn was taken more with the portraits than with the opulence of the house, but his trained eye registered wealth everywhere he looked. He wondered why her uncle had chosen not to be present when they arrived. Bancroft had assured them that he had passed along their plans to arrive before noon.

On the second floor Morna turned down a wide hall that led to the east wing of the house and a suite of rooms that opened in a crescent shape around a large sitting area.

"This is the master bedroom," Morna said in clipped tones as she led the way into a spacious chamber with a monstrous bed at one end and a huge fireplace at the other. "We cleared out everything of a personal nature from the closets and drawers. I think you'll find all the rooms turned out in good order."

"I'm sure we will," Carolyn answered in the same impersonal tone. She was used to dealing with officious nurses and certainly wasn't going to let the housekeeper get the upper hand this early in the game.

Carolyn surveyed the bedroom, which was beautifully furnished in antique furniture that must have been in the family for years. Rich brocaded drapes framed tall windows, and the carpeting was scattered with Oriental rugs. One thought was uppermost in Carolyn's mind as her gaze passed over the one bed with its massive carved headboard.

Where is Adam going to sleep?

She was relieved when she saw him disappear through a door at the far end of the room. There must be an adjoining room of some kind.

"Will there be anything else?" Morna asked.

Carolyn turned to the housekeeper. "No, thank you, Morna. We'll manage just fine."

"None of the household will be home for lunch. Buddy is out in his boat, and Lisa is attending some doings at the country club." Her tone made it clear that preparing lunch was not on her agenda.

"Well, then, I guess there'll just be the two of us for lunch," Adam said, overhearing her as he quickly came back into the room. "We'll wander around for a bit and then find our way downstairs."

An angry flush mounted Morna's throat, but she managed a nod. Her hazel eyes gave both of them an unappreciative once-over, then she turned on her heel and left.

"Brrr," Carolyn whispered with a mock shiver. "That icy look went bone-deep. Don't you think we should have gone easier on her? Given her the day off or something?"

"Household staff can be bullies if you let them," he warned. "If you don't watch out, you'll be waiting on them. Stand your ground, honey."

Honey. The endearment caught her off guard. *Get a grip,* she told herself. A lot of people threw that word around. It didn't mean anything.

"I wish they'd left some of my grandfather's things. Everything looks so…so impersonal." She looked at the huge bed and frowned. "It's almost high enough to need a footstool and wide enough for four people."

"How about two?"

She swung around to see if he was kidding. He wasn't. Her mouth suddenly went dry.

"What are you saying? We're not sleeping together," she said flatly.

"I'm afraid we are," he replied just as firmly. "But only in the literal sense."

"You're serious," she said in disbelief.

"The quickest way for someone to tumble to the truth about our marriage is telltale signs of separate sleeping arrangements. Of course, both of us will have to be on the honor system,'' he added with a grin. ''And you'll have to promise to stay on your side of the bed.''

How could he make light of such an impossible situation? Just the prospect of his virile body lying warmly next to hers fired her hormones in a way she'd never felt before. Did he sleep naked? What if she turned over and felt his inviting body pressed against hers?

''What about the adjoining room?'' she asked. It wasn't that she'd ever had the luxury of a lot of space for herself. She lived in crowded foster homes growing up, and at the hospital, she was used to both male and female interns bedding down on cots in the same room whenever they could snatch some rest. But that was different from sharing a bed with a stranger who happened to be pretending to be her husband.

''That room's a small study,'' Adam told her.

''Well, if there's a couch, I can sleep on it,'' Carolyn informed him. ''The bed in my apartment is narrow and most of the springs are broken.''

As she started toward the door of the study, he reached out and stopped her. ''I'm sorry, Carolyn, but we can't take a chance of someone coming in and finding us sleeping separately. There's too much at stake here.'' He put his hands on her shoulders. ''I promise you that the sleeping arrangement will be strictly platonic, nothing more.''

She wanted to believe him, but common sense mocked the sleeping arrangement. How could they maintain a business relationship in such intimate closeness as sleeping together? Still, what choice did she have? None. Again she admonished herself to get a grip. She'd agreed to do everything she could to make this marriage pretense a success. After all, she'd known that there would be demands that would challenge her determination to hold firm until Adam succeeded in his investigation.

"Okay," she agreed, and forced a smile. "But no swiping of covers."

"I promise."

He was about to drop his hands from her shoulders when there was the sound of muffled footsteps in the hall. He let his hands slip to her back and draw her close, so they appeared to be in a loving embrace when Mack knocked hesitantly on the open door. A short, squarely built man, he had a ruddy complexion and round face.

"Sorry," he mumbled. "Morna told me to bring these things up."

"Yes, thank you," Adam said, keeping his arm around Carolyn's waist as they faced the man. "Your wife told us you're the groundskeeper."

"The landscaping is beautiful," Carolyn offered. "I glimpsed some lovely gardens as we drove up. I can hardly wait to take a walk around. I'm afraid I don't know all the names of flowers and trees that you've planted, but I can tell you have a green thumb."

A pleased flush stole up his cheek. "Thank you, ma'am." Then he nodded his balding head and lumbered out of the room without saying more.

"Nice going, Carolyn. I think you may have gained a supporter there."

"I meant what I said." She didn't like Adam's inference that her remarks had been calculated.

"I know. That's what worries me a little. You

have a tendency to always say what you mean. And in this situation it could be dangerous. Don't take anything at face value,'' he warned. ''Don't trust anyone.''

She glanced at the bed. ''I won't.''

He laughed then, fully and deeply.

LUNCH WAS SERVED ON A flagstone terrace outside large French doors at the back of the house. A shy Asian girl quietly brought them a delicious mandarin salad, hot potato rolls and a whipped fruit dessert. They learned that her name was Seika and that her father, Mr. Lei, had been recently hired as a cook; his two daughters were housemaids. The three were new on staff apparently, and Adam wondered if this change of staff had been Della's decision, and why.

As soon as dessert and coffee were served, Adam leaned closer to Carolyn across the small round table. ''Request a second cup of coffee and linger at the table as long as you can. It's time for me to take a look around.''

Carolyn bit back a demand to know what he was going to do. She knew she'd have to get used to his acting without her knowledge and approval, but it wasn't easy to accept the fact that he would probably keep her in the dark about a lot of things. Still, it made sense not to trust her with any information that she might, inadvertently, blurt out.

Adam quickly left the table and slipped through one of the open French doors. As he followed a hall that led to the front of the house, he passed several open doors, revealing a beautifully furnished room within. When he passed a dining room with a high ceiling and crystal chandeliers, he saw Morna at the far end of the room, by the butler's pantry.

Grateful that she had her back to the door, he slipped by the open door without being seen and hurried up the main staircase. From an earlier report, he knew that Jasper, Della, Lisa and Buddy occupied the wing opposite the one that contained the master suite he and Carolyn had been given. It was pure luck that they were all out for the day. He wanted to get a feeling about these people, and giving their living quarters a quick scrutiny might prove helpful.

As he entered the rooms occupied by Jasper and Della, it was obvious they were cohabitating. Her stuff was mingled with his in the style of a married couple. They each had their own walk-in closet, and judging from the clothes hanging there, both seemed fairly conservative, if quality conscious, in their choice of attire.

Adam was much more interested in an adjoining study, which was obviously a home office and had its own exit into the hall. A large executive desk held the latest and most advanced computer system. Everything needed to transact business was right there in this room, and it appeared from notes and memorandums lying on the desk that Della spent many hours sitting there.

Speculation instantly filled Adam's mind. What programs did she have running? Would they help in his investigation of Horizon? Was there time to log on— These questions came to an abrupt halt as muffled voices floated down the hall.

Someone was coming!

He stared at the door to the hall and prayed they wouldn't use it. Their voices came closer. A man and a woman. Damn. Jasper and Della had come back.

"We have no choice, Jasper. You know that," Della was saying. "It doesn't matter what we think of her. Nothing can be done. We've got to look ahead and see what opportunities may come our way. I can't believe Arthur put one over on us like this."

A low grumble was his only reply.

"Morna says they're having lunch on the terrace," the woman continued. "We'll take a minute to freshen up and then go down with smiles on our faces."

Adam let out his breath when they turned into their private rooms, giving him a chance to ease out into the hall. He couldn't go back the way he'd come without going by their open door. Should he chance it? He had to get back downstairs and join Carolyn as quickly as possible before Della and Jasper made their appearance on the patio.

They'd left the bedroom door open, and he could hear movement inside the bedroom. If he tried to pass the door, one of them might see him.

Deciding not to chance it, he headed in the opposite direction down the hall. As he passed rooms obviously occupied by Lisa and Buddy Denison, he glanced in. The young woman's bedroom was stark white with burgundy accents and filled with designer furniture. Buddy's was that of a young man who chose comfort over style and was cluttered with mementos of his various pastimes: boating, golfing and tennis. The idle rich. These two young people had the lifestyle down to a T.

There wasn't any sign of back stairs at this end of the hall, which Adam had counted on. Only two doors. The first one he tried opened to a linen closet, but as he opened the second one, he breathed, "Bingo."

He knew that in these old mansions, back stairs, or servant's stairs were a must. It was important that staff members serve their masters without cluttering up the main halls and staircases.

When Adam closed the upper door behind him, he was in the dark, except for a thin light coming under the door at the bottom of the stairs. Musty air in the passage made him doubt that it was still in use, and he feared that the door at the bottom might be locked. When he reached it, his hand curved around the old doorknob, and it resisted his pressure, but at last the door opened with a squeak.

He saw that a narrow passage in one direction led to the kitchen, the other to a narrow outside door. No one was in sight as he quickly let himself out of the house and hurried toward the back terrace.

He was congratulating himself on making it back to Carolyn unseen when he realized that she was no longer sitting alone at the table.

A young man with curly chestnut hair that stuck out from under his captain's cap occupied the chair next to her, and both of them looked up when he came into view.

As Adam came toward them, he knew the moment had come when the curtain was going up on a very dangerous pretense.

Chapter Five

Carolyn had been about to get up from the table and return to their suite when her attention was drawn to a white cabin cruiser coming across the water with a foamy wake, and heading for the mansion's private boathouse and dock.

She watched as the craft eased into a berth, and a young man emerged from the cabin. After tying the bow line, he came sauntering up the path with a leisurely gait.

Carolyn knew instantly who he was. Buddy Denison. From the few things Adam and Bancroft had told her, she had already formed an impression of him. He was a young man who sponged off his mother and filled his time pursuing his own interests. Boating must be one of them, Carolyn thought, as he approached the terrace. He was medium height, well-built, and his light brown eyes rounded as he saw Carolyn sitting there, watching him.

"Well, I'll be. It's the rich girl, herself. Mom told me you'd be here today." He gave her an embarrassed grin. "She warned me to make myself presentable. I guess it's too late now."

His relaxed manner put her at ease. "You look

very presentable, Buddy,'' she assured him, nodding approval of his fashionable whites. ''I'm Carolyn.'' She extended her hand.

He wiped his hands on his trousers before taking it. ''Nice to know you…I mean…'' He faltered, obviously searching for the right greeting for someone who might boot him out of the house at any time.

''It's a weird situation, isn't it?'' she said, truthfully. ''Please sit down.''

''Is it really true you're a doctor?'' he asked as he plopped into the chair that Adam had vacated. ''You don't look like one.''

''I only just graduated,'' she said lightly. ''That's a nice boat you have.''

He instantly brightened. ''She's a honey. The Suncrest doesn't go with the house. She's mine.'' There was a warning in his tone. ''You can't take her.''

Before Carolyn could respond, their attention was drawn to a movement below the terrace as Adam suddenly appeared from around the corner of the house.

''I see you found some company while I took my walk,'' Adam said pleasantly as he took a chair opposite Buddy.

''This is my husband, Adam Lawrence,'' Carolyn said. Relief that he was back made her reach over and impulsively squeeze his hand. ''Darling, Buddy was just telling me about his boat.''

Where the conversation would have gone from there, she didn't know, because his mother's voice intruded into the conversation. ''Buddy, I didn't know you were back. I thought you said you'd be out all day.'' Della stepped out onto the terrace.

"No, that's what *you* said *your* plans were. What brought you back early?" He grinned at her. "Couldn't wait to see for yourself what the rich girl looked like, I'll bet."

"Mind your manners, Buddy." Before she could say anything more, a startled gasp jerked everyone's eyes to the doorway behind her.

A tall, thin man with slightly stooped shoulders stood there, staring at Carolyn as if he'd seen a ghost. As he walked slowly toward her, he breathed, "Dear God in heaven, it's little Alicia, all grown up."

Carolyn quickly stood. "Uncle Jasper?"

There was such a fullness in her chest she didn't know if she could keep breathing. He was searching her face with an intensity that seemed to bore into her very soul. Della seemed ready to say something to break the weighted moment, when he sighed heavily. "It's true, then, what Arthur believed? You're Alicia's child?"

Carolyn nodded and tried to find words to tell him that she was as stunned as he was to learn she was his sister's child.

"Where have you been all these years? And why did your mother break our hearts the way she did?" His tone was pointedly accusing, as if years of rancor had finally found a release.

"I don't know anything about my mother except what I've been told," Carolyn responded firmly, lowering the arms she had been prepared to put around her uncle in a hug. His glare didn't invite any expression of joy or acceptance. Just the sight of her seemed to ignite a long-simmering fire, and Carolyn thought with an edge of bitterness that maybe her birthright was something she would have been better off without.

Della moved forward, purposefully edging Jasper to one side. "Carolyn, I'm sorry we weren't here to greet you and your husband."

Adam was ready to jump in and protect Carolyn from both Jasper and Della, if need be. He decided that Della was a woman who was making the best of being fifty. Her dark hair was fashionably cut, curled and colored. Her eyebrows had been precisely thinned, her lashes darkened with mascara and her bold mouth shaped by glossy lipstick. A simple tunic dress was cut in straight lines that flattered her thickening figure. There was a commanding presence about her that warned Adam to be on his toes.

"I'm Della Denison," she said as her dark eyes settled on him for the first time.

"I bet they already know who you are, Mom," Buddy said, his light-brown eyes sparkling in obvious enjoyment of the little scene. "It's my guess there aren't any surprises in this little gathering. We're all just one happy family, aren't we?"

He winked at Carolyn as if sharing a private joke with her, and in a way she was grateful for his inappropriate, juvenile behavior. At least it was honest.

"I'm sorry if seeing me has distressed you, Uncle Jasper," Carolyn said, giving her attention to him, instead of to his paramour. "I know this situation is a difficult one. I wish we could have met while my grandfather was still alive."

"I can't believe Arthur kept such a secret from me," he lamented. "Even though my sister, Alicia, and I weren't very close—there was a ten-year age difference—I still deserved to know."

"He didn't say anything about having found me and providing me with financial support through medical school?" Carolyn prodded. She was anxious to find the tiniest thread of connection between her and the man who had made her his heir.

"Not a word," Della answered in her curt way before Jasper could say a word. "But that was just Arthur. I worked for your grandfather for nearly ten years and was always finding out things he was trying to keep secret. Of course, this situation tops them all." She didn't bother to hide the resentment in her tone.

"Easy, Mom," Buddy said with an apologetic look at Carolyn.

Della ignored her son. "Arthur had a habit of not letting the right hand know what the left was doing. Believe me, it wasn't easy trying to keep things running smoothly in the company when he kept holding things back."

"Arthur never interfered in my lab," Jasper said as if he felt the need to defend his father. "He liked the way I handled everything."

"Then why didn't he leave you fifty-one percent of the shares, instead of only thirty-nine? You were his son, after all." Her tone was bitter.

"It doesn't seem right, does it," Adam said, deliberately fanning the fires. "I wonder why he didn't."

"He was a sentimental old fool, that's why," Della answered, ignoring the fact of Jasper's miserable record of business failure and bankruptcy. "And Carolyn is going to realize in short order that

Horizon needs more than sentiment to keep it afloat.'' Then she added pointedly, ''Of course, there's no reason for her to get involved in the running of the company. It's very demanding. I'm sure the two of you have plans of your own.''

Carolyn and Adam avoided looking at each other. Della had unwittingly hit the truth right on the head. They did have plans of their own, but certainly not the kind this controlling woman expected.

''I want to familiarize myself with Horizon,'' Carolyn said smoothly. ''Because of my medical background, I have an interest in the pharmaceutical industry. Of course, I don't intend to immediately try and run the company, but I think my husband may be of help in pointing out some ways to improve production.'' She gave Adam a sugary-sweet smile. ''Why don't you tell them, darling?''

As Jasper and Della listened to Adam explain his background as an efficiency expert, their hostile resistance was almost palpable.

''So you see,'' Adam finished in an eager voice, ''I've put all my other commitments on hold while I gain some helpful insights on Horizon and make some professional recommendations.''

A tense muscle flickered at the corners of Della's mouth. ''Your work sounds impressive, Mr....''

''Adam, please,'' he corrected her lightly.

''To be honest, Adam, there's no need for that kind of streamlining at Horizon. Our production and shipping departments are running very smoothly, and I think it would be a mistake to alter them.''

''I don't want anybody fooling around in my laboratory, telling me what to change,'' Jasper said flatly. "Especially someone who doesn't know a beaker from a Bunsen burner."

Adam laughed, trying to ease the tension. "I can appreciate your position, Jasper. You don't have time to waste on someone who isn't knowledgeable, who lacks the training to see what you're about."

"Well, I'd love to see your laboratory," Carolyn said smoothly, stepping into the opening, knowing Jasper couldn't very well fault her medical background. "It will be an opportunity to educate myself even further in laboratory research."

Nicely done, Adam thought, pleased that Carolyn used her status as a medical doctor to eliminate any of Jasper's objections to her presence in his workplace.

Conversation faltered, and only Buddy's quiet chuckle broke the silence.

"We thought it might be appropriate for us to invite a few people over this evening," Della said, giving Carolyn and Adam a smile that didn't reach her eyes. "Just a casual get-together. Mostly staff from the company. We didn't want to rush things, but since we really didn't know your plans, we thought that knowing a few people might ease the situation a little. The grapevine has been thriving since the news broke that they have a new boss."

On the surface it seemed like a friendly gesture, but Adam was wary and suspicious. Did Della have some hidden agenda behind it? He knew that Carolyn would hate the idea of being on display and meeting a bunch of people, but as far as his investigation went, there might be a few fringe benefits in the affair.

"You'd better put on your battle gear, Carolyn,"

Buddy warned with a grin, ignoring his mother's razor-sharp glare.

LATER, BACK IN THEIR WING of the house, Adam and Carolyn sat on a couch in the small study, talking quietly. She was trying to still the nervous fluttering that just thinking about the evening ahead caused. She felt like someone holding on to a swiftly moving raft, not knowing what lay around the next bend.

"Why do you think Buddy said something like that?"

"Probably because he knows that his mother is a possessive dragon when it comes to anything connected with Horizon. Della doesn't want you—or me—invading her territory. Because Jasper's interest and attention is centered in the laboratory, your grandfather gradually put the business end of the company in Della's capable hands. It's obvious Della feels very 'mine' about the whole thing."

"Then how are you going to get by her to do any investigating?"

"My wife is going to override her objections." Sitting so close to her, Adam was aware of every breath she drew. His reaction to the tantalizing scent of her perfume and the teasing softness of her fair hair, surprised him.

Wife. Carolyn stiffened. She knew that the term meant nothing to him, but it made her uncomfortable. "And how is your *wife* to do that?"

"She's going to exercise her authority."

"I don't know if I can do it. I need time. Time to adjust, to learn, get my bearings."

"Time is what we don't have," he answered

firmly. "Not if we want to stop illegal shipments as quickly as possible."

She sighed, and he fought the urge to draw her close and have her nestle her head against his chest. He'd shut down his feelings after he'd lost Marietta, and the stirring of sensual desire startled him. He feared that at any moment, he might ruin everything, betray her confidence in him, by a simple word or gesture.

"Why do you suppose Della invited people over to meet us on our very first night?" She searched his face for reassurance that it made some kind of sense.

"Who knows?" *Probably to throw you off balance.*

"I'm scared," she admitted. "What if I make a bunch of mistakes and blow everything?"

Adam knew that what he was asking of her would have challenged a tough, experienced agent. She was not totally unaware of the danger in the situation, but he had hesitated to dwell on the risks because he didn't want her living in fear.

He'd purposefully avoided talking about her grandfather's death. Until he knew whether the hit-and-run was deliberate or otherwise, he'd keep his own counsel. Increasing her fears and apprehension would be counterproductive. Handling the curious staff from the company that Della would parade through the house that evening was a challenge he knew she could handle.

"Maybe it's better to face them all as soon as possible," he said, trying to put a positive spin on the evening. He knew that the meeting with her uncle had not gone as Carolyn hoped. She'd been ready to receive Jasper with love and affection, and he'd only focused on the disappointment he'd felt over his sister's behavior. Resentment simmered behind almost everything her uncle had said to her. Obviously her inheritance was a red flag to Della, and Adam didn't doubt for a minute that the war had just begun.

"I don't have anything suitable to wear," Carolyn startled him by saying.

This sudden shift in perspective caused Adam to impulsively put his arm around her shoulders and give her a squeeze. "Whatever you decide to wear, you'll look ten times sexier than any woman there."

She stiffened slightly, and he knew he'd used the wrong adjective. Carolyn obviously didn't think of herself as sexy. But maybe she should. Had she ever enjoyed her sexuality? Been in love? Even as he asked the questions in his mind, something deep within him didn't really want to know.

As it turned out, he found out the answers a lot sooner than he'd expected.

CAROLYN STOOD WITH ADAM in the main drawing room as a dozen guests circulated, smiling, laughing and speaking in low tones as they sent surreptitious glances at the couple. Seika and her sister, Lotuse, circulated with drinks, while a sober-faced Morna kept her eye on the lavish buffet.

Carolyn hated being on display as much as she'd expected. Even Adam's admiring eyes as he nodded approvingly at her yellow summer dress had not boosted her courage much. He matched her casual attire in tan slacks and an open-neck shirt that pulled across his shoulders and chest in an attractive way.

He had a pleasant smile for everyone. Carolyn had never been with a man who was so at ease with strangers. He possessed a compelling energy that seemed to draw everyone's nodding approval as he smiled, shook hands and bent his head to listen carefully to what someone had to say.

When he openly demonstrated a possessive affection toward his wife, Carolyn felt herself responding to his charm on a level that frightened her. His endearments—sweetheart, darling, my love—were like seeds falling on fertile ground.

Steady, girl. Steady. This was no time for dangerous fantasies. It was all a pretense and he was very good at it, she reminded herself.

The way he seemed able to hold on to the names of people that came up to introduce themselves amazed her. To Carolyn, it was all just a vague procession. There was no one who really interested her until Lisa Denison breezed into the room, still wearing her tennis whites.

Della gave her daughter a horrified look, which Lisa ignored. The young woman was petite, curvaceous and pretty enough to grace the cover of any magazine, and Carolyn had the instant impression that Lisa Denison made her own rules and to hell with anyone else.

"So you're Arthur's big surprise," she said, crossing the room to greet Carolyn. "How lucky can you get? I bet you never thought something like this would happen to you." Her mouth parted in an honest grin.

"I'm still pinching myself," Carolyn conceded. Maybe it was because Carolyn suspected the young woman had deliberately left on her short-skirted tennis outfit to annoy her mother, but for some reason, this simple act seemed to put them on the same side. There weren't many people that Carolyn instantly liked, but Lisa Denison was one of them. She found herself smiling back at the vivacious young woman.

"And you must be the surprise husband," Lisa said, giving Adam a deliberate once-over, then she smiled and nodded with approval.

"That's me," Adam responded with a grin that matched her saucy attitude. "Pleased to meet you, Miss Denison."

"Well, all I've got to say is that Carolyn is twice lucky," Lisa declared, with an airy laugh. "You two being here should perk up this dull place. Maybe I'll stick around a little more. Of course, you'll probably be living too high to spend much time at this mausoleum. There are things to see and places to go." She gave them a petulant frown. "What's the use of having money if you don't know how to spend it?"

"I agree," Carolyn said, much to her own surprise. She would have bet that her former impoverished state wasn't a secret. "Maybe you can show me the best places to shop? I'm going to need some female input on a lot of things."

"I'm the one." She eyed Carolyn's slim figure and simple dress with a knowing smile. Then she winked at Adam. "You won't know her when I'm finished with her."

With a wave of her hand, she made her way to the buffet and started flirting with a young man there.

"Good job," Adam whispered. "You set that up beautifully."

"I did?" She hadn't even thought about their hidden agenda. In reaching out for Lisa's friendship, she had been simply following a spontaneous impulse. What if she continued to act impulsively and made serious mistakes that could endanger their lives? Suddenly she felt a little ill.

As more people came up and introduced themselves, she concentrated on making noncommittal responses to their curious questions about her role in the company. She was wondering how soon she could make an escape when a tall young man with short, bleached-blond hair approached her with a drink in his hand and a knowing smile on his face.

"Just like old times, Caro. The last time I saw you was at a party."

"Cliff Connors," she gasped in surprise. Of all the people in the world who might show up at the Stanford mansion, Cliff certainly wasn't one of them. He'd been a medical student in her third-year class and had had all the marks of becoming a scientist, but he'd fouled up.

He laughed at her astonishment. "Yep, it's good old Cliff."

Carolyn introduced him to Adam. "We were in the same study pod and hit the books together. It was a rough year for all of us."

"What she's trying to say in a nice way is that I flunked out. And my farewell party was a bash I'll never forget." He chuckled. "Who would have thought we'd both end up here? I've been Jasper's laboratory assistant for a year now, and here you are, ready to take over the company. How lucky can I get?" He winked at her. "I could use a raise."

"Well, I'll see what I can do," Carolyn answered, playing along.

"It's great to see you land in clover. I never knew anyone who deserved it more. I heard that Dr. Meyerson left his wife finally." He glanced at Adam and then back at Carolyn. "Though I guess it's a little too late for him to reap the benefits."

"It was always too late," she responded evenly. But she was clenching her hands so tightly that her nails bit into the flesh. She went cold all over, and then, in the next instant, turned hot with an anger she thought had died long ago.

"We'll have to get together sometime and talk about old times." Cliff's smile seemed innocuous enough, but an unspoken implication lingered as he turned away.

Adam could tell from the way the pulse in Carolyn's neck throbbed that she was fighting for control. He slipped an arm around her waist. "Darling, let's duck out for a while. With luck, we might not even be missed."

She nodded and let him usher her quickly to a side door from which a few steps led down into a sheltered garden.

Keeping his arm around her waist, they followed a curving path away from the house. They could hear Buddy's boat rocking gently against the dock, and somewhere upstream a stereo was sending music across the water. The setting was tranquil, and Carolyn nodded toward a nearby garden bench

Her face was white in the glow of moonlight and her lips quivered with emotion as she quipped, "Well, that was fun, wasn't it?"

"Do you want to talk about it?" he asked quietly.

"No, I don't want to talk about it. I don't want to think about it. I..." Her voice faltered. "I want to forget what a fool I was."

"All of us are fools at one time or another. I'm afraid that's what life is all about."

"I thought all the pain had gone. But it's still there." She stared up at the sky for a long time, then she began to tell him what had happened during that third year of medical school.

As Adam listened, he thought the story was commonplace enough. Dr. Eric Meyerson was a good-looking, thirty-five-year-old teaching professor. He probably picked out a vulnerable female student in every class who was receptive to his ardent attention.

Carolyn was a perfect target. She was without family, fighting her battles alone, and starved for someone to love her.

"I guess I knew down deep that Eric was leading me on, but I desperately wanted to believe that someone really cared for me. When I was with him, it seemed possible that he would leave his unhappy marriage for me. Then I would have a home, a real home." She gave a choked laugh. "All that happened was an abrupt end to the affair when a new class of students arrived. He told me that he and his wife had reconciled. I guess she finally got tired of his lies. Anyway, I learned my lesson. End of story."

"Is it? If the mention of his name can keep you locked in the past, the bastard wins." He frowned. "Tell me about this Cliff guy. Did he know about the affair?"

"Yes. He caught us one night in Eric's office. But

as far as I know, Cliff never told anyone. The study pod was the only contact I had with Cliff. He was very smart, but always a kind of a cutup. No one was surprised when he dropped out. Why do you ask?''

''His not-so-casual mention of the doctor seemed like some kind of a setup. Now that I know the story, I wonder...do you think he's capable of blackmail?''

She swallowed hard. ''I don't really know. He didn't spread the story around while he was in school.''

''Now that you've come into money, he may have a different idea about keeping quiet.''

Her lips trembled, but she said firmly, ''He's mistaken if he thinks I'll run scared.''

''Good.'' Adam lightly cupped her chin and turned her face toward his. He wanted to kiss her in the worst way, but settled for a light touch of his lips to her forehead. ''I heard some advice that helped me when I needed it. The past is accepted. The future is open.''

''Thank you,'' she said softly. ''I'll remember that.''

They sat for a few more minutes in comfortable silence. Then he asked, ''Are you ready to go back to the party, Mrs. Lawrence?''

''Yes, Mr. Lawrence.''

Grateful for his warm, strong body brushing hers as they walked slowly back to the house, she let herself pretend for a moment that she was living a romantic dream.

Chapter Six

Carolyn lay on her side of the mammoth bed, wide awake and staring at the ceiling. She could hear Adam's even breathing across the wide span of mattress between them. Earlier, when she'd nervously prepared herself for bed, she'd lingered in the bathroom as long as she dared. After a quick shower she had dried and brushed her hair until it fell in natural ringlets around her face.

A foolish fluttering in her stomach mocked the "business arrangement" of sleeping in the same bed with an almost complete stranger. What did she really know about Adam Lawrence? Practically nothing! He'd admitted that he had created a fabric of lies to cover his real identity. How much of what he had told her about himself was really true? The little bit of personal history he'd shared with her could also be a fabrication. Somehow he'd managed to get past her usual emotional defenses and had stirred feelings in her she'd been denying for a long time.

All evening she'd played the role of a woman in love, staying at Adam's side as they mingled with the guests. He had showered her with adoring looks and murmured endearments. She'd seen the way other women looked at him, and she'd felt a ridiculous pang of regret that none of his adoration was for real. Now she faced the challenge of sleeping in the same bed with him. Could she trust herself? Could she trust him?

As she'd stared at her reflection in the bathroom mirror, her hands nervously smoothed the collar on her pajamas and smoothed a wayward tendril of hair into place. Suddenly her hands froze in midair as an inner voice mocked her.

What on earth are you doing? Getting ready to sleep with your pretend husband?

She'd choked back a nervous laugh. Taking herself in hand, she shoved aside the foolish thought that this was her wedding night. Maybe the only one she'd ever have.

As she quietly eased out the bathroom, she was relieved that Adam was still in the adjoining study, and she was surprised when she heard him talking quietly to someone on his cell phone. Who was he calling this time of night? Curious, she paused and listened as his deep voice floated through the open door into the bedroom.

"That's what I love about you, Angel. You always know how to…"

Carolyn closed her ears to any more. She'd felt like a fool as she climbed into bed. He had a sweetheart. Or a wife. Apparently the woman was someone who understood the nature of his work. Everything he'd said about this being a business arrangement was true. His gentleness and kindness had had nothing to do with romantic feelings. How could she have let herself even think for one moment that he might be attracted to her? She was probably as safe in bed with him as a nun in a convent.

When he'd turned out the light and eased into his side of the bed, she'd pretended to be asleep. When he'd quietly said, "Good night, Carolyn," she'd known she hadn't fooled him. But he had laid down the rules, and she would play by them.

SHE AWOKE IN THE MORNING to find herself alone in the bed. The bedside clock read six-thirty, and she sighed wearily, knowing that the day was going to be a demanding one. Adam had warned her that her first visit to Horizon would not be easy.

Where was he? She listened, but couldn't hear any telltale noises that he was still in the suite. He must have dressed and left when she was still asleep.

She stayed in bed for a few minutes longer and nourished a spirit of rebellion. She was in charge of her own life, wasn't she? Why couldn't she decide what she was going to do and when she was going to do it? Why was she letting him orchestrate her every move as if she were some kind of puppet?

Carolyn had never been one to lie to herself. The truth was that nothing had changed since she'd been so shaken up by the sick baby and the sample medicine from Horizon. She knew that her own feelings were not top priority in this situation. If she could save the life of a single person, she had no choice but to stay the course until Adam's investigation was successfully over. Sighing, she threw back the covers and made ready for her first day at the company her grandfather had left in her care.

When she got downstairs, she found Adam sitting with Jasper in a breakfast nook off the kitchen. A beautiful antique sideboard offered a breakfast buffet, and Morna was checking the silver tureens filled with food.

"Good morning, darling," Adam greeted her as he stood up and put a loving arm around her shoulders. From the tiny tightening at the corner of her mouth, he could tell that she was forcing a smile. When he had eased into bed with her last night, he'd sensed her withdrawal, and at the time he'd thought it was just the unconventional situation. Now he wasn't so sure. She was as rigid as a store mannequin under his touch.

Jasper rose to his feet in gentlemanly fashion, and Carolyn quickly took a chair next to his. Her uncle's eyes narrowed as he looked at her. "I still can't believe it."

"Neither can I," Carolyn responded readily. "I never imagined that I'd be sitting here, having breakfast in a lovely home like this with my uncle."

Jasper's narrow face softened a little. "I guess Arthur decided to give us all a surprise. He was a man who decided how things should be and then made sure they turned out that way." The resentment in his voice was obvious. "Several times I wanted to leave the company, move out of the house, but he always managed to make sure that didn't happen."

"Have you always worked at Horizon?" Adam asked as if he didn't have background reports verifying that Jasper had failed at his own business and depended on his father for his job. Adam wanted to find out how deep the bitterness ran. Why would Jasper remain in his father's home, instead of moving out with someone like Della? It didn't make sense unless there was a hidden benefit.

"It was my father's plan all along that I become a scientist at Horizon. We have one of the best research laboratories in the country. Of course, I could have gone to another company, anytime, for more money."

"Why didn't you?"

Jasper's long, bony fingers tightened on his cup. "There were reasons." His flat response did not invite any more of Adam's questions.

"More coffee?" Morna asked Jasper as she hovered near his chair. "Another piece of toast?"

Adam couldn't help but notice the housekeeper's solicitous manner toward Jasper. Morna's almost pleasant expression was a change from her usual glower. Adam had noticed a marked difference in her the minute Jasper had walked into the breakfast room. Inconsistencies in behavior always captured Adam's attention. Morna was about the same age as Jasper, and Adam wondered if she'd been in the house since he was a young man. When Della walked into the breakfast room, Morna's glower was back.

"Good morning," Della said briskly as she nodded at Carolyn and Adam. "I'm surprised to see the two of you up so early. I hope you slept well."

"Very well," Carolyn lied, hoping that makeup hid the dark circles under her eyes. She was used to long hours at the hospital during her internship and had managed to function well on very little sleep. The emotional load that Cliff had dumped on her and the revelation that Adam had an "angel" in his life created a different kind of tiredness.

"Thank you for the nice reception last night," Adam said as he held out a chair for Della between his and Jasper's. She wore a navy blue two-piece dress that softened her middle-aged figure. Her makeup was carefully applied, highlighting her hazel eyes and widening her lips.

She turned to Morna to give her order for breakfast. Then she reached over and patted Jasper's hand. "I thought you might want to stay home today and rest, dear. You were up and about most of the night."

When he didn't answer, Della turned to Carolyn. "Sometimes Jasper spends half the night poring over his notebooks and charts. He never tells anyone what he's working on until he's sure of the results." There was a warning in her tone as she added, "I hope you're not going to put pressure on him to share anything until he's ready."

"I'm sure Uncle Jasper and I can develop a satisfactory relationship at work and at home," Carolyn replied smoothly. In medical school she'd learned how to handle people who insisted on telling everyone when to jump and how high. Della's forceful manner didn't intimidate her a bit. She was confident she could handle the challenges of the business world, but her personal life was another matter.

Her eyes slid to Adam as he leaned back in his chair. He looked perfectly at ease in his fawn-colored slacks and open-neck shirt. He grinned at her as he caught her appraising eye.

"Darling, would you like another blueberry muffin? I know they're your favorite." Adam's tone was intimate and suggestive, as if they were talking about something more private than muffins.

"Thank you, love," she answered, masking an honest reaction to his attention. He lied so well it almost took her breath away. He was good, she had to admit. The way his gaze was centered on her, the lingering touch of his hand as he handed her the muffin and his suggestive wink could have sent her emotions reeling if she hadn't known that his behavior was nothing more than professional pretense.

She turned to Della. "Will Lisa and Buddy be joining us for breakfast?"

Jasper snorted and Della gave a short laugh. "Only if we label lunch as breakfast. They're night owls. Jasper and I leave for work at eight o'clock most mornings, and we don't see the children until the evening meal at seven."

Children? Carolyn was surprised Della used that term, but it seemed to verify her suspicion that Della was the one responsible for keeping her son and daughter dependent and spoiled. Carolyn couldn't help wondering why her grandfather allowed Della and her grown children to sponge off of him. Maybe Arthur had figured he owed Jasper this chance at domesticity.

"And what are your plans for the day?" Della asked brightly as if Carolyn and Adam were visiting guests with a tourist agenda.

"When would be the best time for us to drop by Horizon?" Carolyn asked, implying that she valued Della's opinion. "Since we're all up and ready, maybe we should all go in together this morning?"

Adam resisted putting a hand over his mouth to hide his smile. If he'd ever had doubts about Carolyn's ability to subtly take charge of a situation, they were gone now. She'd deftly put Della in the position of having to go along with her suggestions or appear antagonistic.

"Well, yes, I guess that would be all right, but you might get a better feel for the place later on in the day," Della said. "Mornings always start kind of slow, you know."

"Really? Then that might be the best time to wander around and see what's happening. What do you think, darling?" she asked, tossing the ball to Adam.

"Great," he answered enthusiastically. "Honey, I guess we might as well confess. We're both workaholics," he told Della and Jasper. *You may as well get used to seeing us every time you turn around.* Aloud he said, "We'll try to stay out of your way, though. We don't want to interfere with your regular routine."

Della looked at him as if to say, *Aren't you doing that already?*

JASPER AND DELLA DROVE their own car, a black Lexus, with Carolyn and Adam in the back seat. As they swept through the gated community, Adam could tell that Carolyn was overwhelmed by the display of wealth. Her posture was stiff, and she gave every appearance that she was headed for some unbearable ordeal. Last night, when he'd come to bed, she'd looked so tiny, curled up on the far side of the bed, he'd wanted to ignore the promises he'd made to keep his distance. He realized that she had only accepted his support during the evening gathering because she was caught off guard by Cliff.

When they'd retired to their room, she showed a little nervousness, but this morning her behavior had been distant and guarded. Was she troubled about his knowing her personal affairs? Cliff Connors had really thrown her a curve last night, and she probably had every right to be worried about his intentions. Not only could he be a potential blackmailer, but he could be up to his neck in a black-market scam.

Carolyn's efforts to act the loving wife at breakfast would have fallen flat if anyone had been paying close attention, but fortunately both Della and Jasper seemed to be too caught up in their own world to notice.

As she stared out the car window, he moved closer, slipped his arm around her shoulders and whispered, "It's going well. You're doing just fine. Remember, today you're just a visitor. You don't have to do or say anything that doesn't feel right."

A slight nod was her only response.

As her hair brushed his cheek, a faint scent of rosewater teased his nostrils. Her ivory complexion was soft with a hint of light powder, and her lips were shaped by a kissable pale pink lipstick. Everything about her invited a man's loving touch, and he fought the impulse to follow through on the desire surging through him. His voice was suddenly husky as he whispered, "Nothing's going to happen to you. I promise to keep you safe."

She turned and looked at him with a wan smile on her lips. "I know you will. You're the best."

When they reached Horizon Pharmaceuticals, located south of downtown Seattle, their car was promptly admitted through the security gate. Jasper drove to a designated parking area and then motioned for them to follow him and Della into the first building through a private security entrance.

Two twin brick buildings were joined by a second-floor skywalk, and the grounds were circled with a security fence. Only the front business entrance was open to the general public.

ADAM KEPT HIS ARM through Carolyn's as they walked. The trepidation she was feeling in seeing her inheritance for the first time was registered in the quickness of her breath and the pulse visible in her slim neck. He was certain she was caught up in an aura of total disbelief.

"All the main offices are on the first floor. And there are two rows of cubicles for the business staff," Della told them, then pointed out a long reception desk just inside the front entrance that kept any visitors in the small waiting area. She explained that identification tags and approved clearance were necessary to enter any other section of the two buildings.

"Arthur's office is at the end of the main corridor, and mine is next to his." She motioned toward an elevator. "Jasper's laboratory is on the second floor and connects to the second building, which houses the production, packaging and shipping departments. What would you like to see first?"

"My grandfather's office."

"I'll be upstairs when you get around to the laboratory," Jasper said as he punched the elevator button. It wasn't the most gracious invitation, but the older man gave Carolyn a weak smile that softened his briskness.

Della spun on her heel and led the way down a private hall. Carolyn was surprised there wasn't a secretary sitting at the desk outside her grandfather's office. When she asked about it, Della said that Arthur's secretary had retired after many years of service. The brisk way she said it made Carolyn wonder if the woman's retirement had been by choice.

Della unlocked the door to the office, and a lingering scent of pipe tobacco greeted them as they entered. Carolyn's gaze settled on the large leather chair behind the executive desk. The cushions were shaped by long use, and in her mind's eye she could imagine her grandfather sitting there. The desktop was cleared except for a phone and pipe rack. As she looked around the room, there was little to give her a feel for the man who'd occupied this office for so many years.

As if reading her thoughts, Della said briskly, "We cleared out the office after Arthur's passing. His computer and files were moved into my office. Most of his personal things were packed up and taken to the house. I see that we forgot his pipe rack." Her mouth quivered slightly as if she was fighting back some emotion. "You could always tell where Arthur had been by following the scent of his tobacco."

"I'd like to look through his things sometime," Carolyn told her. "And also the personal items from his bedroom."

"Of course," Della said readily. "I understand."

"And please bring back his computer and business files."

"Oh, I'm sure I can provide you with any information you need. You'll never be able to get a true overview of the company without some personal direction." Della's expression had changed, as had the timbre of her voice. She was no longer the accommodating employee.

"We'll certainly be needing your help, Della," Adam said smoothly. He wasn't surprised at the change in attitude. If Arthur had left any clue as to what was going on at Horizon, it might be in his personal files. "We know you're busy and have a heavy responsibility. Whatever we can do on our own will relieve you in time and effort. I'm sure his computer files would be a help."

Della must have heard the determination in his voice, because she gave a short nod and said, "All right, I'll have someone move his computer back. Now, you will have to excuse me. I'll alert all the department heads that you are on the premises. I'm sure that some of the staff you met last evening will be happy to show you around."

"Thank you, Della," Carolyn responded. "We really appreciate what you've done to make us welcome."

"I wouldn't start stirring too many pots, if I were you." With that warning, she left the office and closed the door with a punctuating bang.

"Ouch!" Adam said. "I guess we know how she feels about us being here."

"Do you think she knows the real reason we're here?"

"Most people view any kind of change as trouble. Della could be as innocent as a snowy-white lamb and still be resentful of our presence. Or she could be damn worried that we'll turn up evidence that will bring the law down on her neck." He set his mouth. "It really doesn't matter. We'll do what we have to do."

"I'm not sure what that is," she admitted as she surveyed the large paneled room. An area for conversation—a brown leather couch facing two chairs—had been set up at one side of the office, near large windows. She walked around the room, hoping to somehow draw in the essence of the man who had spent so much of his life there.

"Why don't you check the desk drawers and see if they cleared them out?" Adam suggested, realizing she needed something to do.

"What am I looking for?"

"Anything that might be in Arthur's handwriting. I'll tackle the cupboards. And I ought to check the built-in bar," he added with a grin.

Some of the tension left her face as she smiled at him. "Yes, you'd better do that—but not till after lunch."

They spent the morning searching the office until Adam was finally convinced that nothing the least bit informative remained in any of the drawers and cupboards. If there had been anything that would point to illegal activities in the company, the evidence was gone now.

No one interrupted them during the morning, the phone didn't ring, and the missing computer and files were not returned. He couldn't very well force the situation without alerting someone to his hidden interest in the company. Forcing himself to be patient was going to be a challenge.

"What now?" Carolyn asked, disappointed on several levels. She didn't find anything that would give her a personal glimpse of her grandfather, nothing that gave her an overview of the company and certainly nothing that Adam found of interest.

Adam glanced at his watch. "What do you say we break for lunch? We passed a small seafood restaurant just down the block. We could get a bite to eat and then wander upstairs and pay Jasper a visit."

Carolyn's first impulse was to say, no, she wasn't hungry. She knew that once she stepped out the door, she'd be on display again. An ever efficient grapevine had undoubtedly spread the news that she was in the building.

Adam teased her. "What would you prescribe in this situation, Doctor? A lengthy fast or an indulgence of good food and drink?"

His ability to make her step out of herself and laugh surprised her. Instead of increasing her anxiety, his chiding gave her a strange kind of reassurance. She picked up her purse. "Who's buying?"

He laughed. "My rich wife."

He opened the office door and waved her out with an elaborate gesture. There was nothing she could do but straighten her back and walk out into the hall. Della's office door was closed.

Carolyn breathed a sigh of relief when they made it out the private entrance without running into anyone. As she walked to the restaurant with Adam, she enjoyed a sense of victory that she'd made it through the first morning without any disasters. With Adam at her side, she almost felt invincible.

That feeling was shortlived.

A few minutes after they'd entered the restaurant and given their orders to the waitress, Carolyn's stomach plunged and she lost her appetite.

"Oh, no," she breathed as Cliff Connors walked into the restaurant. Her hope that he might not see them faded. His casual stride was purposeful and his smile fixed as he walked directly toward their table.

Carolyn tasted bile as she steeled herself to face the threat Cliff represented. The memory of the night he'd intruded on her and Eric's intimacy came back with a wash of embarrassment, now mixed with fear. Even though Cliff hadn't spread the tale at the time, she suspected he'd kept his silence because she knew of his involvement with one of the pregnant nurses. The scales were balanced then, but not now. She realized that money would outweigh anything she could bring against him. What if Adam's speculation was true? If Cliff spread the sordid tale to the tabloids, her reputation would be ruined. What was the alternative? If she gave in to a blackmailer at this point, where would it end? Her mouth went dry.

Chapter Seven

Adam turned his head to see what had caused all color to drain from Carolyn's face. "Easy does it," he cautioned her when he saw Cliff coming toward them.

"Hello, Caro. Long time no see," he said, grinning at her and Adam. "Good party last night."

"Yes, it was," Adam answered smoothly, giving Carolyn time to collect herself. "It was nice of Della to arrange the gathering. We're looking forward to spending more time with the staff."

"I heard you were in the building this morning. I guess you'll be wandering up to the lab to take a look."

"Maybe after lunch. Would you be available to show us around, Cliff?" Adam smiled broadly as if he was looking forward to the idea of seeing more of him.

"I'm your man. Anything I can do to ingratiate myself with the boss is my style, right, Caro?"

"I don't know, is it?" she asked without blinking.

Cliff laughed. He seemed a little taken back by her blunt question, as if he hadn't expected her to take his flippant remark seriously. "You'll have to step lively to keep up with this wife of yours," he told Adam, and started to say something more when he was interrupted by a tall, too-thin young woman who appeared at his side.

"I'm sorry, I'm late," she told Cliff, slightly out of breath. "I got held up in packaging. Someday the Dragon Lady is going to push me too far."

Cliff gave her a warning look. "I don't think you want to bring Della into this conversation, Susan. Meet Horizon's new owner, Dr. Carolyn Leigh Lawrence."

"Omigosh." Susan put a hand to her mouth, and her plain features reddened with embarrassment. She looked almost ill as she stammered, "I'm...I'm sorry. I didn't know. I—"

"I told you you should have gone to the reception last night, Susan," Cliff chided.

"I'm not very good in a crowd," she said to Carolyn.

"It's all right," Carolyn said quickly, trying to ease the situation. "To be honest, I met so many people last evening I'm not sure I'll remember half of them. This is my husband, Adam Lawrence."

"I'm Susan Kimble. Nice to meet you both," she responded, seeming more flustered than ever. She wiped nervous hands on her brown slacks and sent Cliff a beseeching look. "I work in the business office, and sometimes Cliff and I have lunch together. Don't you think we'd better find a table?" she asked him as if anxious to end this embarrassment.

Cliff waited just long enough to decide that no invitation to join Carolyn and Adam was forthcoming, then he nodded and smiled at the attractive waitress who arrived with Carolyn and Adam's order.

"We'll see you later then," he said as he guided Susan to an empty booth.

"That was enlightening, wasn't it," Adam said in a matter-of-fact tone as he reached for a roll.

"What do you mean?"

"Sometimes it's amazing how easy it is to learn things without even trying. We know that Della's nickname is Dragon Lady, which isn't surprising. And then there's Susan. Not exactly a femme fatale. You have to wonder what Cliff's motive is for taking her out to lunch." He eyed Carolyn as he bit into the roll. "Any ideas?"

"She has something he wants?"

"Good guess. It might be interesting to find out what that is. Maybe she's just an easy score, but I wouldn't bet on it. Even though she seems to lack sophistication, I wouldn't be surprised if there's more depth to her than shows."

Carolyn marveled at Adam's detached perspective. He seemed to have the ability to look at everything and everyone as if separate from his own feelings. *Like our pretend marriage.*

The unbidden thought brought a strange kind of regret. Logically she should have been grateful that he was handling this almost impossible situation so impersonally. She'd let herself fall in love once, but now that her life was spinning off in a different direction, she didn't need a man to fulfill it, certainly not one who was already taken. The warmth that coiled within her when Adam touched her and called her sweetheart was a weakness she would have to overcome. If all went well, she'd probably never see him again after this was over.

"What are you thinking?" he asked softly, leaning toward her. "Do you know your blue eyes turn to a lovely shade of midnight when you're deep in thought?"

The caress in his voice startled her. They weren't on display now. There was no reason for him to play the loving husband. A shock of dark hair had drifted down on his forehead, softening his strong features, and there was a sensitivity about him that was totally disarming and appealing. She didn't doubt for a moment that more than one woman had responded to his masculine appeal, and it didn't surprise her in the least that he had found someone to fill the emptiness his wife, Marietta, had left.

"I was just thinking about Susan," she lied, then added, truthfully, "She doesn't look as if she's the type to play the mating game the way some girls do. I'd like to warn her about Cliff. He has callously dumped more than one young nurse."

Adam gave his attention to the tasty avocado hamburger, while he silently wondered if the connection between Cliff and Susan was based on matters of the heart or something more mundane like money. And what was Cliff's relationship with Della? He'd jumped on Susan fast enough when she referred to Della as the Dragon Lady. He kept such speculation to himself and tried to keep the topic of conversation general.

Carolyn played with her spinach salad as she made superficial responses to his light conversation. Silently she wished she could still drive her own old car and head back to her cramped apartment. She wasn't ready for this. If Adam hadn't pushed her into this dangerous charade, she could have taken all the time she needed for a smooth and easy adjustment.

"What's the matter?" he asked, catching her frown. "I have the feeling I'm not rating too high as a luncheon companion. Maybe we could get better acquainted. You know, pretend this is a first date."

The irony made her laugh. They'd slept in the same bed last night and were committed to a dangerous agenda, but she didn't know much more about Adam's personal habits and preferences than her mailman's. Maybe less. She knew the bald-headed postal carrier loved sports and saw every Seattle Seahawks' home game, and she didn't even know if Adam liked sports. Books? Movies? Television? Any of the mundane things that brought two people together? But what did it matter? They had to stay focused on more important things, such as finding out if her grandfather's death was an accident or a deliberate act.

Adam watched her eyes shadow and her mouth tighten. He knew that the brief moment when they might have enjoyed a respite from the impending pressures was gone.

She laid down her napkin and shook her head when the waitress inquired about dessert. Adam picked up the bill and they walked out of the restaurant together, his arm around her waist as if they were the newlyweds they pretended to be.

Horizon's research laboratory was on the second floor of the first building. Sterile conditions were enforced, and Carolyn and Adam were provided with masks, latex gloves and disposable plastic lab coats. Carolyn was used to hospital procedure, and so the personal protective equipment and speaking in muffled tones from behind a plastic mask felt natural to her. She was silently amused at Adam's awkwardness and obvious discomfort. In some of the isolated sections, the technicians wore paper lab suits, hats, boots, gloves and masks. Her uncle Jasper appeared in sterile garb and quickly conducted them through the research laboratory.

He made no effort to explain what experiments were being conducted as they passed long lines of black-topped benches and work areas. Numerous computers and printers were in evidence on the counters, and Carolyn knew that much of the lab equipment was automated for both input and output.

Jasper set a pace that gave Carolyn little time to pause and see clearly what the laboratory assistants were doing, but she had no intention of letting her uncle shut her out of his department. Various chemicals and substances mingled to create a distinctive lab odor, and she decided that she'd insist on being briefed on the research projects later.

She didn't recognize anyone from the gathering the night before. Jasper nodded to an office with windows on one side of the office. His name was embossed on the door. There were a few desks at the end of the rows of benches for the techs in the lab, and Carolyn saw Cliff's name on one of them. Jasper led them out of the lab on the far side, where they discarded their sterile garb.

"The production and packaging departments are in the next building," he said as they passed through a glassed-in breezeway that connected with the second floor of the adjoining building. "And the shipping department is below, on the first floor."

They passed through security doors and entered the production room, which was painted the same white as the laboratory. Personnel wore white uniforms, plastic caps and masks. A hum of various machines and conveyor belts created a kind of factory ambiance as containers were filled with all kinds of pharmaceuticals.

He introduced them to Nellie Ryan, the department head, whose windowed office provided a view of the busy production floor. Adam remembered her from the gathering at the mansion the night before. She was a large, freckled woman with a firm handshake. Her smile seemed genuine as she greeted them.

Jasper shifted impatiently as she bragged about the efficiency of her department and readily answered questions from both Carolyn and Adam.

"We have a sign-off for anyone who handles the containers of pills, capsules and liquids," Irene explained. "Every lot is labeled and can be tracked with expiration date and lot number. All the controlled substances, such as morphine, are under constant monitoring, and the people working with them are kept isolated in a contained area."

Jasper seemed to have little interest outside his own realm, and Adam could see why Arthur Stanford had decided not to leave Horizon in his hands. Carolyn asked pointed questions and nodded in understanding. Her astute and inquiring mind would have pleased her grandfather, Adam thought. He could see her taking the reins of the company and successfully acting as its CEO—if the black marketing of Horizon's drugs was stopped before disaster hit the company.

Jasper hurried them into the packaging department next, obviously disgruntled with his role as tour guide. He made no attempt to use the occasion to get closer to Carolyn. If anything, he treated her presence like an unwanted intrusion. Della must have coerced him into doing the tour, Adam thought, knowing he'd have to make his own inspection later.

A brisk matronly woman, Elinor Forbes, was the packaging manager. She nodded at the introductions and shook their hands politely, but the first words out of her mouth made it clear that this was her domain and she didn't brook any interference. She'd been with the company for almost twenty-five years, and Arthur had left her some company stock in his will.

Elinor quickly explained the packaging process, the weighing of contents, labeling and signing off of shipments as they were boxed for delivery downstairs to the shipping department.

Adam listened carefully to her explanation of how the orders were filled. In every department he'd been trying to analyze how the illegal activity in the company could be done. He finally reasoned that if he could identify fraudulent shipments and then backtrack to where the orders came from, he had a chance of identifying who was masterminding the operation.

They thanked Elinor for her time, and then Jasper suggested they finish the tour in the shipping department on the first floor.

As Jasper introduced them to Nick Calhoun, the

shipping manager, Adam thought he detected some undercurrent between the two men. Neither of them exchanged any pleasantries, but maybe that was just Jasper's usual distant manner. He seemed to have little interaction with anyone outside his laboratory. Still, it could be a front, Adam reasoned. Jasper might have been screwing his father big time, knowing that his chance to inherit the company and property was a long shot.

"I'll leave you to look around," he told Carolyn and Adam as he left them in the shipping department and made a hasty retreat back to his laboratory.

Nick Calhoun was a stocky man with a round, ruddy face and a ready smile. "Ain't you the pretty one," he told Carolyn, giving her a frank appraisal. "Imagine that. Arthur's long-lost granddaughter. I never would have believed it. But here you are." His eyes twinkled at Adam. "You got yourself a gold-plated wife, that's for sure. Sorry I didn't get up to the house to meet you folks last night. My poker-game buddies don't take my absence lightly." He shook his balding head. "They took me for twenty bucks, though. I guess I should have accepted the Dragon Lady's invite." He didn't hesitate to use the unflattering nickname.

"If I'd had half a chance, I would have missed the gala affair myself," Adam confided with a friendly grin. "A poker game sounds a lot better."

"Maybe you'd like to join me and the boys sometime?" Nick offered with a speculative glint in his eye.

"Sounds great. Okay, sweetheart?" Adam asked in husbandly fashion.

She nodded agreeably, knowing exactly what he

was up to. The deception didn't sit easily with her. She hated to manipulate people, and Nick seemed like a nice man, friendly and sincere. Adam was playing him and she knew he was depending on her to keep the doors open for his investigation, so she swallowed the bad taste in her mouth.

"Will you show us around, Mr. Calhoun?" she asked.

"Nick," he corrected her. "Sure thing. I think I'm going to like having a new boss lady. And a pretty one at that." His bushy eyebrows raised in approval as he grinned at her. Then he turned to Adam. "I hear you're some kind of efficiency expert. We could probably use some of that."

With the air of a commander-in-chief, Nick walked them through the busy loading dock area where trucks were lined up, waiting to be loaded with boxed orders waiting on racks of iron shelves for delivery. Then he took them into his small, crowded office and showed them the delivery schedules.

Adam asked some pointed questions that didn't resonate with anything in Carolyn's background. She knew nothing about the intricacies of transporting merchandise. As far as she was concerned, the post office was the way and means of sending anything. She realized with a sickening feeling that without Adam alerting her, the illegal traffic in black-market drugs would have gone on right under her nose.

"Do you handle all this paperwork yourself?" Adam asked, shaking his head. "I'd think you'd need a secretary or two."

"Can't find good help," Nick said flatly. "Once

in a while we hire someone to catch up on the filing, or Nellie comes down after hours and gives me a hand. She's a whiz on the computer.''

Adam picked up something in the man's tone that indicated the pair had more than a business relationship. Nick's next words confirmed it.

''Nellie was at the shindig last night. Nellie Ryan. You probably noticed her. She's got freckles and a smile bigger than all-get-out.''

''We just had a nice visit with her upstairs,'' Carolyn said. ''She's a nice woman, and seems to have the production department running smoothly.''

''You'd better believe it. Nothing gets by Nellie. She's got a sixth sense that'll drive a man crazy. I ought to know. We've been dating on and off for a couple of years now. She's one smart lady.''

''And I bet she has a good disposition to put up with you, Nick,'' Adam teased.

Nick grinned as he tucked in his shirt over his ample belly. ''Well, we get along pretty good. Say, why don't you two drop by the Galloping Goose after work? We could lift a few beers and get better acquainted. A lot of the workers at Horizon stop in there before going home.''

''Sounds good to me. We'd like that, wouldn't we, honey?'' Adam said before Carolyn had time to think of a polite refusal. Hanging out in a smoke-filled bar wouldn't be her favorite way to pass the time, but he didn't want to miss the opportunity to mingle. Tongues got looser with every bottle of beer. Nick's congeniality and being seen in the Irishman's company might grease the hinges on some other doors for him.

"Sounds lovely," Carolyn lied with a forced smile. "I look forward to it."

"Wait'll I tell Nellie we're going to down a few with the boss lady herself." He winked at Adam. "This place is looking up."

They left the shipping department and made their way back to the other building. Carolyn didn't say anything about the impromptu beer date until they were back in her office.

"Was that date with Nick necessary?" she asked as she dropped down onto the leather couch, and leaned her head back against the cushion. "I've never liked going to bars. The smell of beer turns me off, and after I've had a couple, I just want to go somewhere and sleep."

He laughed and sat down beside her. "I'll remember that and make sure you end up in the right bed."

She knew he was being facetious, but his nearness was a poignant reminder that if she couldn't hold her booze, he would be the one to put her to bed.

As she turned and looked into his arresting face, she was startled to realize that the thought was not all that displeasing. Maybe she was just feeling off balance and needed a shoulder to lean on. She was tired of going it alone all the time. What did she care if he had someone he called Angel waiting in the wings?

"I'm game," she said.

"I think your education has been sorely lacking if you've never been to a bar and done Karaoke," he said, letting his arm slip behind her.

She chuckled. "I'd never be able to get up in front of people like that."

"You don't know what you're missing. It's great

fun. You might enjoy seeing me make a fool of myself sometime.''

"Yes, I would," she said with an honest laugh. "That would be fun." *Fun.* The word sounded strange on her lips. What if they had met under different circumstances? Would she have let herself relax enough to have fun with someone like him?

"It's a date," he said as if they had all the time in the world for such frivolity.

The growing intimacy was broken by a brisk knock on the door, and Della entered with some computer disks, followed by a thin, round-shouldered man in overalls carrying a computer. "Sorry, we didn't get this back to you sooner," Della said briskly. "I've been going in three directions all day. In fact, I really haven't had much time to even check Arthur's files. Everything is still the way he left it."

Adam instantly wondered if she was telling the truth. The fact that she kept her eyes from contacting either his or Carolyn's was suspicious. People lied better when they didn't have to look at someone.

"I suppose you'll want this on the computer stand next to the desk, Carolyn," she said in a tone that indicated she expected Carolyn to be changing things around at the first opportunity.

"That will be fine," Carolyn replied, and added just as pointedly, "For now."

Adam suppressed a grin. *Good for you, Carolyn.* Once she got her feet on the ground, she'd be able to hold her own with the Dragon Lady. In fact, Carolyn ignored Della and turned around to smile at the man as he settled the computer, printer and files in their places.

"Thank you for the help," she told him.

"Glad to meet you, ma'am. Bob Beavers."

"It's nice to meet you, too. This is my husband, Adam Lawrence."

The man wiped his hand on his overalls before holding it out to Adam for a shake.

Della gave them an impatient look as if taking time for such niceties with a maintenance man wasn't on her list of priorities. She turned to Carolyn. "I imagine you'll want to schedule some kind of staff meeting. You'll have to let me know in time to clear the docket. Any extra demands put an overload on everyone."

"There isn't any hurry, is there? I mean, none of us are going anywhere, are we?" she inquired innocently as if Della might have other plans in the works, like leaving the company.

Della was obviously taken aback, and Adam could see fear in the tightening of her facial muscles. It was almost as if she realized for the first time that she wasn't in the driver's seat anymore.

Adam wasn't sure that putting her on the defensive was a good idea—people struck out when they had their backs to the wall. He couldn't help but wonder if Arthur had put her in that position and lost his life over it.

Della moistened her lips. "What are you suggesting, Carolyn? If you're insinuating that I don't intend to stay at Horizon under the present circumstances, you are totally wrong."

Her manner and voice indicated to Adam that the woman was willing to do whatever necessary to keep her present position and power.

Della gave them a forced smile. "Horizon is my life."

"That's a relief, Della," Carolyn said quickly. "I can't imagine the chaos if you were to leave us." She shuddered. "I don't even want to think about such a thing."

Good girl, Carolyn. Adam breathed a little easier. They didn't want to stoke any dangerous fire. They needed time to ascertain where the smoke was coming from. Maybe Della was innocent. And maybe she wasn't.

After Della returned to her office with Bob Beavers in her wake, Adam turned to the computer. "Well, let's see if this baby has anything to say. You want to take a look?"

Carolyn shook her head. "The computer at the investment company where I worked was friendly because I knew the programs. I made use of the school computers for my studies, but I'm like someone trying to get upstream without an oar when you throw anything new at me." She made a flourishing gesture at the computer. "It's all yours."

While Adam sat mesmerized in front of the monitor for the rest of the afternoon, Carolyn went through material put out by Horizon, which gave some empirical data about the company's commitment, its history and research. Her admiration for her grandfather grew as she began to glimpse the legacy he'd left her. It saddened her to think that someone had twisted her grandfather's ideals into something ugly, and her resolve strengthened. She would prove that she was worthy of his trust, no matter what personal sacrifice she had to make. She was filled with a desire to learn everything she could about all the operations here and the people who were responsible for carrying them out. Writing down questions that she wanted answered gave her a sense of moving forward into her new responsibilities, and she was hopeful that her growing knowledge of the company would help Adam in his investigation.

As her gaze wandered to him, she realized that giving up his companionship was going to cost her more than she'd ever imagined. Already he'd moved into a space in her heart that had been empty, even during her ill-fated infatuation with Eric.

Restless, she wandered over to the computer. Leaning over his chair, she was aware of the scents of shampoo and aftershave. She placed her hands on his shoulders and felt the warmth of his body and the hard cords of muscle. An undefined desire spiraled through her. She remembered the times he'd had his arm around her, pretending to be the loving husband, and wished that his embraces could have been for real.

Stop it! Your heading down the wrong road, girl. Aloud she said, "Well, what do you think?"

"Everything seems routine, but I've selected a few disks to send to the agency's system-analysis experts so they can take a look at them. As far as I can tell, there's nothing here to show any irregularities in the production and shipping of the pharmaceuticals but we know for damn sure that someone is manipulating the system. All we have to do is find out how—and then we'll know who."

"Is that all?" she teased.

He reached back and captured her hands where they lay on his shoulders. "What do you say we call it a day? It's almost 'happy hour.' Shall we wander down to the Galloping Goose and relax?''

"Sure, why not?" she said, hiding a foolish disappointment as he turned off the computer and stood up.

"I'm ready for a break."

The intimacy she'd felt touching his shoulders was gone. He wasn't going to the bar to relax with her; he was going there on business. He was sticking to the game plan, and that was a good thing, she told herself, but what was wrong with enjoying the illusion that they were a happily married couple?

She slipped her arm through his and gave him a smile that caused one of his dark eyebrows to lift in surprise.

Chapter Eight

The Galloping Goose was a saloon and café, fashioned with a timber ceiling, portholes for windows and a profusion of anchors, ropes and driftwood scattered about on the walls. The kitchen was labeled The Galley. Waitresses were dressed in short, white dresses with middy tops, and when they bent over tables, panties decorated with anchors were revealed.

The building was on the waterfront and flanked by popular marinas, and the clientele seemed to be a mixture of working people and affluent boat owners.

A Seat Yourself sign seemed to set the casual tone of the place. Adam put a guiding hand on Carolyn's arm as they made their way along the side of the room to a booth near one of the portholes. Music blared from an adjoining room, and a small dance floor was visible through the open double doors. Several couples were dancing.

A hefty barmaid, with a sailor's hat perched saucily on her brassy-blond hair, approached Carolyn and Adam as soon as they were seated.

''What's your poison?'' she asked tritely without

giving them a menu. Apparently eating was not high on the list of customer priorities.

Adam ordered draft beer and Carolyn decided on a margarita.

No sign of Nick and Nellie. *Maybe they aren't coming,* Carolyn thought, not knowing whether to be disappointed or relieved.

"Shall we order something to eat?" Adam asked, peering at plates of seafood and steak being served at other tables.

"I wouldn't dare. Morna advised me this morning in no uncertain terms that dinner would be at eight, and asked if we would be dining at home. I assured her that we would be. I don't want to get off on the wrong foot with her. Della would never forgive me if Morna up and quit."

"I don't think there's any danger of that," Adam said, remembering the way Morna hovered around Jasper that morning. He'd bet anything there was a history between those two. "Well, then, how about a dance to help me forget my hunger pangs?"

Carolyn hesitated. She'd never had a chance to learn a lot of different dance steps, but she could hold her own with most partners. There was one intern at the hospital who was very good, and he always danced with Carolyn when they had staff parties. She was curious to know how Adam handled himself on the dance floor.

Very nicely, as it turned out. With perfect ease he guided her steps in rhythm with a ballad about true love. He held his head so close to hers that laying her cheek against his was a given.

They stayed on the dance floor for several numbers. There was an unspoken communication between them as they moved together, and a demanding warmth began to surge between them. Carolyn ignored the warning that what was happening deep within her was no pretense, no playacting. When sexual desire, like a simmering Roman candle, was ready to ignite, she came to herself with a jolt. What kind of signals was she giving? She'd be a fool if she invited this kind of love-play and then expected him to stay on his side of the bed.

She withdrew from his embrace and said rather breathlessly, ''That's enough.''

She turned quickly and found herself face-to-face with Cliff Connors.

''Whoa,'' he said. ''I was hoping to cut in before the song ended. How about it?'' He gave Adam a wink. ''You don't mind my taking the little lady for a few turns around the floor, do you?''

''Your timing is bad, Cliff. We were just about to sit down,'' Adam replied in a pleasant tone, but one laced with enough firmness to make Cliff back off.

He shrugged. ''Well, maybe another time. How'd you discover my favorite haunt, anyway?'' His tone implied they had deliberately followed him there.

''We heard it was a popular place for people from Horizon,'' Carolyn answered. From the way Cliff was crowding her, forcing his company on her, she knew that sooner or later, she was going to have to deal with him.

''Let's finish our drinks, darling,'' Adam said, ''and then head home.''

Cliff hesitated as if about to force his company on them, but must have thought better of it. ''Well, then, have a nice evening, you two. I'm sure we'll connect another time."

It sounded more like a promise than an idle remark. He sauntered over to the bar and joined a group of young people, laughing and talking.

Carolyn finished her margarita in a leisurely fashion and shared with Adam some of the questions she'd written down while going through the company's printouts. They ordered a second round of drinks, and Carolyn would have felt uncomfortable in the rather raucous atmosphere without a date, but in Adam's company she relaxed and thoroughly enjoyed herself. She couldn't believe how late it was when he motioned for the check.

Cliff had already left the bar, and there was still no sign of Nick and Nellie.

"I guess they changed their minds about dropping in here tonight," Carolyn said. "I bet Nick really didn't expect us to come."

"You're probably right," Adam conceded, disappointed. He hated passing up any opportunity to get close to someone who might offer some insight to what was going on in the company.

As they left the restaurant, the deepening twilight lay silvery patterns on the water, and a light breeze rocked tethered boats like a mother's gentle hand.

Carolyn took a deep breath of the misty air as they walked around the building to a crowded parking lot. She was thinking how much she was enjoying the evening when the sound of groaning stopped them in their tracks.

"Someone's hurt!"

"Over there." Adam spurted between two cars in the direction of the groans.

A man lay on the ground, breath raspy, his limbs doubled up in pain. A high arc light and a sliver of moonlight flickered across his battered face.

"Nick!" Adam cried in surprise.

"Dear God, no," Carolyn gasped as she knelt down beside him. Her trained fingers registered a pulse in his neck. Good. Strong. She quickly assessed the way he was doubled up. The reflex pinpointed pain in his abdomen, and his raspy breath was likely caused by broken ribs. Blood pooled on his bald head.

"Call an ambulance," she ordered as she began to check his limbs. No broken arms or legs.

"We got a man hurt," Adam told the 911 operator on his cell phone. "Galloping Goose parking lot on Cove Street. Send an ambulance."

Nick groaned louder than before as his eyes fluttered open.

"Can you talk to me, Nick?" Carolyn asked as she checked the swelling on his head.

The first audible words out of his mouth were curses. Carolyn had heard most of them before, but never with such vehemence.

"Take it easy, old boy," Adam soothed. Someone had beaten the hell out of the guy, for sure. "Was Nellie with you?"

Carolyn's heart lurched to stop. Had someone beat up Nick and abducted Nellie?

"Talk to us, Nick," Adam coaxed. As an investigator, he knew that time was the greatest element in solving any crime. "Nellie? Was Nellie with you?"

Through swollen, bleeding lips Nick mumbled, "No. Just me."

"Do you know who they were, Nick?"

"Didn't see...clobbered me...from behind."

When the ambulance arrived, Nick was still swearing and clutching his stomach. Carolyn was concerned that some internal organs might have been damaged and gave a quick report to the paramedics.

One of them recognized her from the runs he made to the Friends Free Clinic to pick up a patient who needed to go to the emergency ward.

"Dr. Leigh, you making house calls in parking lots now?" he asked with a boyish grin.

"Anytime, anyplace," she quipped.

He just laughed and quickly loaded Nick into the ambulance. They followed the ambulance at a slower pace to the University of Washington Hospital. By the time they got there, Nick was already on a stretcher and inside.

Carolyn's professional status gave her immediate access to what was happening. The examining doctor's findings were very much what Carolyn had determined, and he ordered immediate diagnostic tests to determine any internal injuries.

"I'm going to call Nellie Ryan," Adam told Carolyn when she returned to the waiting room. "She's listed in the telephone directory, and I think she should know what's happened to Nick. There's always a chance that she may be able to shed some light on this whole thing."

When he closed his cell phone after talking to Nellie, he said, "She's on her way."

Twenty-five minutes later, Nellie burst into the emergency waiting room, flushed and breathless. Now that she wasn't wearing a cap to cover her hair, they saw that she was a fiery redhead. "What kind of accident did Nick have? Is he all right?"

Adam knew from Carolyn's sharp glance that she was startled he'd labeled Nick's beating an accident. He'd purposefully given Nellie the wrong impression because he wanted to witness her reaction when she learned the truth. Maybe the woman's surprise would be honest and maybe it wouldn't. The fact that Nick had showed up at the Galloping Goose alone, instead of with her, might mean something.

Adam watched her carefully when he explained that Nick had actually suffered a vicious beating. Her gasp of "Oh, no," could have meant anything. His gut feeling told him that Nellie Ryan wasn't totally surprised.

"The doctors are determining the extent of his injuries now," Carolyn offered as Nellie dropped into a chair and stared at the floor.

Adam sat down beside her. "Do you have any idea who might have done this, Nellie?"

She was silent for a long moment, and Adam didn't know if she was carefully fashioning a lie or was hesitant to tell the truth. Finally she said, "It's his gambling. He's been losing—a lot. I guess someone is trying to collect."

"He must be in pretty deep," Carolyn murmured as if Nellie's explanation made perfect sense to her.

Adam wasn't so sure. Nick could have been roughed up because of default on a gambling debt. On the other hand, he could have been beaten as a warning not to talk about what he knew was going on at Horizon.

When the doctor came in to report on Nick's injuries, the news was good. No serious damage. Just bruises, contusions and no sign of concussion from the blow on the head.

Nellie hurried up to his room to see him, but Carolyn held Adam back when he was preparing to follow her.

"You can talk to him tomorrow. He'll be in better shape then."

And more prepared with any lies, thought Adam, but he didn't argue. He could tell that Carolyn had had more than enough for one day. She glanced at her watch as they left the hospital.

"Almost ten o'clock," she groaned. "Della and Morna are going to be furious. We should have called. I didn't even think about dinner."

"Do you want to stop someplace and get a bite?"

"I don't think so," she answered. "Not if you're courageous enough to raid that huge refrigerator with me."

"I'll be behind you every step of the way," Adam promised solemnly.

She laughed, and they began to tease each other about who was going to face up to Della if they got caught sneaking out of the kitchen with a chicken leg in each hand.

They slipped into the house like conspirators and she stilled a foolish impulse to giggle. Feelings that took her totally by surprise made her feel young, almost giddy. Nothing in her wildest dreams had prepared her for sneaking into her own wealthy mansion on a mission of stealing food for a late-night picnic.

The main floor was dark except for several night-lights, and the kitchen was in shadow except for a hanging light over the central work area. They peered into the refrigerator and checked covered containers until they found the makings of roast beef and turkey sandwiches.

Carolyn was surprised at how deftly Adam threw the sandwiches together while she collected some fruit and chips. She was debating about something to drink when Adam took the decision out of her hands and lifted a bottle of wine from a wall rack.

They were about to congratulate themselves on their accomplished thievery when they were caught red-handed. They heard someone at the back door, and before they could make their escape from the kitchen, Buddy walked in.

He flipped on the overhead light as if about to do some night raiding of his own. "Well, well, for shame," he said, a grin spreading across his face. "And what do we have here? Lovers satisfying a bit of hunger in the middle of the night?

As heat surged into Carolyn's face, her first impulse was to deny the smirking insinuation that they had sneaked down to the kitchen after a bout of lovemaking.

Fortunately Adam had no trouble sidestepping the remark. "Is that why you're here? You've been out working up an appetite yourself?"

Buddy laughed in a good-natured way. "Let's just say I took my boat out for a midnight run—and I wasn't alone." He winked knowingly at them. "I was here for dinner, though. Mom was fuming because of your no-show, and Jasper was ticked off because he'd had to play tour guide. When the two of them join forces, there's hell to pay. I wouldn't want to be in your shoes, Carolyn."

"I'm sure we can work things out," she answered with more conviction than she felt.

"Well, I hope you're not going to tighten the purse strings," he said frankly. "Mom's a bear when she's forced to turn loose with an extra dollar. Jasper lets her handle all the finances, you know. He's right along with me and Lisa, begging for an extra dollar. I know she's got a nest egg hidden away somewhere, but I'll probably never see any of it till she's six feet under."

The callous remark made Carolyn want to lash out at him about getting a job and earning his own way, instead of waiting for his mother to die.

Adam took a different tack. "I guess Arthur was pretty good to her during the years."

"What she's got, she got on her own," Buddy said bluntly. "Well, I'm beat. See you in the morning—maybe."

Carolyn and Adam looked at each other as he disappeared, but before they could say anything, a movement at one end of the kitchen caught their eyes.

Morna stood, a scowl on her face, in the servants' hallway. Her graying hair was tightly braided, and she wore a faded, unbecoming bathrobe that was pulled tightly over her large figure. To their surprise, she ignored the pilfered food and bottle of wine in their hands.

"Buddy Denison is a lazy leech," she said in a tone that was almost a growl. "Never done an honest day's work in his life. If you want to know the truth, Mr. Jasper has been a saint to put up with him and his sister." Her mouth tightened. "You'd be doing everyone a favor to toss all of them out."

Her tone left no doubt that Della was included in the statement as Morna turned around and disappeared. Carolyn decided she certainly wouldn't want to be in Buddy's shoes if the woman ever unleashed her anger.

These encounters in the kitchen took a toll on Carolyn and Adam's appetite, but they carried their food and drink upstairs to their wing of the house and settled in the study with a pleasant fire.

Adam did his best to recover their earlier light-heartedness, but without much success. Carolyn made a valiant effort to respond to his quips, but he could see it was a strain.

As the firelight flickered on her face, she looked fragile and vulnerable. *What have I done?* he asked himself with a pang of guilt. He wanted to assure her that all would be well, but how could he lie to her? He longed to pick her up in his arms, tuck her in bed and crawl in beside her. A spurt of warm desire picked up the thought, and he forced himself to get to his feet.

She put down her half-eaten sandwich and finished her small glass of wine. "Any plans for tomorrow?"

He sensed that already danger and deceit were thickening around her. She could precipitate some dangerous reactions without even realizing it.

"Why don't you sleep in and give me a chance to check out the business of Nick's? I don't know if his beating is connected to anything going on at Horizon or if it's related to his poker playing."

"I could go to the office without you," she offered in a slightly defensive tone.

"Of course, you could," he agreed. *Easy does it,*

he cautioned himself. He knew she was more than capable of moving ahead on her own, and under normal circumstances he would have applauded her determination to take hold of her inheritance. If he didn't handle her exactly right, she could put herself in jeopardy without even knowing it.

"I was hoping that maybe you could spend some time with Lisa and pick up a little personal background on her mother. There's always the chance that Arthur might have said something to Della, which she repeated to her daughter. A casual remark might give us a hint of Arthur's concerns. Maybe you could do some of that shopping she suggested."

He reached out and helped her to her feet. He had promised her that he wouldn't make any advances on her, and he wondered if she could tell that she was becoming very important to him on a level that had no place in this investigation.

For a moment she leaned into him as if inviting his embrace. He let his arms encircle her back and then stiffened as he felt the vibrating warning that his cell phone was ringing.

Damn. Angel was the only one who had this number. Why was she calling at this time of night? He stepped away from Carolyn and drew out the pocket phone. "Sorry, why don't you head for bed while I take this call?"

Her expression was unreadable, but as she disappeared into the bathroom, she gave the door a punctuating slam. He knew one thing for sure. He would be staying on his side of the bed that night.

Chapter Nine

When Adam left their suite early the next morning, Carolyn was still asleep on her side of the bed, and there were no signs the rest of the household was awake. He slipped out to his car and headed toward town. The late call had been from the agency, giving him the background check on Cliff he'd requested. He found some of the data very, very interesting.

Cliff's father had been a successful oil man and had settled his family in several foreign countries while Cliff was growing up. Cliff's schooling had been varied, and he had attended several universities, earning high marks in a few areas. His medical career had seemed a sure thing until his father died, and then Cliff dropped out of medical school after achieving only certification as a laboratory technician.

The report made one thing clear to Adam. Cliff Connors was one smart fellow. Maybe smart enough to run a black-market scheme right under Jasper Stanford's nose. But Cliff couldn't do it alone, Adam thought as his hands tightened on the steering wheel. He'd bet there was a weak link somewhere, and he intended to find it.

As he passed a coffee shop a couple of blocks from Horizon, he saw Susan Kimble sitting at a window table and quickly pulled into the parking lot for his morning coffee and a chance to see what he could find out about Susan's relationship with Cliff.

"Morning, Susan," he greeted her with a broad smile. "Mind if I join you? I left the house without my usual caffeine fix."

She looked startled and embarrassed to see him, and her hand went to her collar in a nervous gesture. Even as she nodded, he had the feeling she was already getting ready to flee.

"You must be a morning person like me," he said in a light conversational tone. "It's barely six o'clock and here we are. Oh, you're not meeting someone, are you? I wouldn't want to intrude…"

"No, I'm not meeting anyone. I take an early bus and spend time here until the gates open." She looked worried, as if her habit might not have his approval for some reason.

"Sounds like a good idea," he assured her quickly.

Obviously she wasn't used to having coffee with someone she barely knew, but after a few minutes she seemed to relax.

Adam kept the conversation light and general, hoping that she might offer some information about Cliff that might be useful. When none was forthcoming, he mentioned casually, "We saw Cliff at the Galloping Goose last evening after work. I guess that's a favorite hangout."

He was surprised when she said, "I don't know. I've never been there."

"Really?" He searched her face, trying to pick

up some undercurrent of emotion. "You've never been there with Cliff? I mean, the two of you having lunch together yesterday and everything, I kinda thought..." He let his words trail off, inviting her to set him straight.

"Oh, there's nothing like that between Cliff and me." She looked almost pleased that he'd thought such a thing.

Either she was a damn good actress or she was telling the truth. He veered the conversation in another direction. Since the company grapevine would be buzzing with Nick's assault, he might as well view Susan's reaction when she heard the news.

She listened, looked horrified, then made all the appropriate remarks about how awful it was. Only one thing was missing from her reaction—honest surprise. Adam would have bet she already knew.

He decided to go fishing. "Are you friends with Nellie Ryan?"

She seemed surprised at the question. "I know who she is. Why do you ask?"

"She came to the hospital last night to be with Nick."

"I see her once in a while at work, but we're not really friends."

Then who told you about Nick's beating last night?

The question must have flickered in his eyes, because Susan suddenly showed her earlier signs of nervousness. She touched her mouth with her napkin. "I really better be going."

Her hasty exit spoke volumes. His fishing expedition had snagged something, but what? Her defenses had gone up as if he was trawling too close to forbidden waters.

WHEN CAROLYN AWOKE it was midmorning. For a moment she panicked. She'd missed her shift at the hospital by oversleeping. Her loyal little alarm clock must have failed her.

She sat up with a jerk and the elegant bedroom came into focus. Then she remembered. She glanced at the other side of the bed. Empty. Only the impression of Adam's head on the pillow told her that he had slept there. Usually the dip of the mattress under his weight signaled his presence, but last night a bone-deep fatigue had claimed her. She must have fallen asleep before he finished his telephone conversation, because she couldn't remember him crawling into bed with her.

Thank heavens, she thought as she steeled herself to face another day as Mrs. Adam Lawrence. God help her, if she played the fool and let herself believe in the charade of this so-called marriage, if Buddy and Morna hadn't spoiled the mood of their "picnic" and Adam's phone call hadn't come when it had, no telling what would have happened.

As she dressed and made her way downstairs to the morning room, she half expected to see Adam sitting there waiting for her, but only Lisa was at the table, sipping coffee and reading a fashion magazine.

She gave Carolyn a warm smile. "Somebody else knows a civilized hour for breakfast, I see. Terrific. I hate to eat alone." She touched a porcelain bell sitting on the table. "Morna always removes the breakfast buffet right at nine o'clock, but Seika will bring you anything you want.'' She eyed Carolyn's trim figure. ''I'm betting you're a toast-and-coffee gal.''

Carolyn smiled and shook her head. ''I usually prefer a hearty bowl of oatmeal, because when I'm busy, lunch often gets missed.''

Lisa sighed. ''You workaholics are a mystery to me. My mother is the worst kind. She wore my father out with all her push, push, drive, drive.'' She didn't disguise her resentment when she added, ''He ended up six feet under when he was only forty. Heart attack.''

''I'm sorry,'' Carolyn murmured. ''That's young.''

''I guess that's why Buddy and I are determined to have a little fun while we can. Of course, how long that's going to last depends on you,'' she added frankly. ''Are you going to boot Mother out of the company?''

Seika appeared at that moment and Carolyn didn't have to answer. The pretty young woman poured her a cup of coffee and took Carolyn's request for orange juice, oatmeal and toast.

''Well, are you?'' Lisa asked again when they were alone. ''Are you going to give Mom her walking papers and take over?''

Take over? The thought was so scary that for a minute Carolyn didn't know what to say.

''I mean, I could understand your wanting to be the CEO,'' Lisa said. ''I guess that's what Arthur had in mind, making out that unbelievable will to a granddaughter he didn't even know.'' She gave a false laugh. ''The whole thing beats me.''

''Me, too,'' Carolyn admitted honestly. ''Did my

grandfather give any hint that he was disturbed about anything that was happening at Horizon?''

''Disturbed?''

Carolyn knew the question was a clumsy one, and she felt an unreasonable spurt of resentment that Adam wasn't around to smoothly guide the conversation. ''I mean, did he seem to be himself before the accident?''

''I haven't the foggiest idea what was going on in Arthur's mind. He was always pleasant enough, but he didn't have much to do with Buddy and me.''

She eyed Carolyn's plain linen dress, slightly faded from repeated washing. ''What do you say we go shopping? The next best thing to splurging on myself is spending someone else's money.''

''All right. Sounds like fun,'' Carolyn agreed, knowing Adam would be pleased she'd followed his suggestion.

It didn't take long for Carolyn to realize that Lisa had told her the truth—she loved spending money, period. And boy, did she know how to do it, Carolyn thought as they emerged hours later from another expensive boutique with more new clothes than she'd had in the previous five years.

When Lisa suggested they have a late lunch at the country club, Carolyn agreed. With all the shopping, there hadn't been any chance to pump Lisa about her mother or the company. So far, she'd picked up absolutely nothing that might interest Adam. At Lisa's urging, she'd decided to wear a sexy red dress out of the store and wanted to try out her new look on some unsuspecting strangers. Maybe she'd get used to the glances that came her way as the two of them sauntered down the street, loaded with packages.

Highland Country Club guests and staff alike seemed to know Lisa, and she laughed and joked with everyone as she led the way to an attractive patio overlooking the golf course. Carolyn was conscious of curious looks that came her way and she was grateful that Lisa didn't stop to introduce her to anyone. She felt like an actress making her entrance on the stage without the foggiest idea of the script.

Lisa insisted on ordering a couple of cocktails while they consulted the menu. Carolyn followed her suggestion and ordered shrimp-and-lobster salad which Lisa had proclaimed "divinely wonderful."

"So, Lisa, is there a man in your life?" Carolyn asked as they ate. She was determined to glean something worth reporting to Adam.

"I'm dating a golf pro at the moment," she said with a shrug. "I need a change of scenery. Until Arthur got himself killed, Mom was talking about financing a European trip for Buddy and me."

"Really? That would have been nice. Does she travel out of the country a lot?"

"No, but I think she had plans for that to change. I heard her talking to Arthur one night about making some trips to increase Horizon's foreign markets. I don't think he liked the idea." Lisa caught the waitress's eye and ordered a second drink.

Did the discussion have anything to do with illicit black markets?

"I wonder why she wanted to take a working vacation?" Carolyn mused.

Lisa gave a disinterested shrug. "Arthur slammed out of the house and a few nights later he was dead.'' She took a hefty swallow of her second drink. ''That's the trouble with my mother. She thinks business morning, noon and night. I think Arthur got tired of it. You'll get tired of it, too, Carolyn. She'll want to run your life, as well as the business. But you can always depend on me to rescue you.'' She tossed her pretty head. ''I have a feeling I can teach you a lot about living the easy life.''

Carolyn didn't doubt it for a minute. From everything she could tell, Lisa Denison had made a career out of doing absolutely nothing, beautifully.

By the time they returned to the mansion, Carolyn had tired of Lisa's company and conversation. Lisa wasn't at all like Rosie. Carolyn wished she could have explained everything to Rosie, but Adam's conviction that they'd both be in danger if someone tumbled to the truth had kept her quiet.

When Adam called the house at noon, Morna briskly informed him that Carolyn and Lisa had gone shopping. She said briskly that she had no idea when they would be back.

''Will you and Mrs. Lawrence be dining at home this evening?'' she asked. The fact that they'd failed to appear the evening before had been duly noted and chalked up against them.

''Yes, Morna. We'll be staying in this evening.''

He would much rather have had a private dinner with Carolyn at some small, intimate restaurant, but there was no question that duty came first. He'd had a sense of a time clock ticking from the first moment he was given this case. He couldn't ignore any opportunity to observe the people who might be involved in the death of a lot of innocent people. If

Jasper, Della and her children had been unaware of the new will, there might have been a conspiracy among them to get rid of the old man—especially if Arthur had discovered any nefarious dealing in his company.

Feeling this urgency, Adam had spent the day laying the groundwork for more detailed scrutiny of Horizon staff and business procedures. He had arrived early enough to take a look at the shipping department while the loading doors were still closed, and no one had arrived for work yet. Since he knew that Nick wouldn't be showing up for work that day, Adam started with his office.

"Is there something you need?"

Adam turned from the filing cabinets whose contents he'd been about to examine and saw Nellie standing in the doorway. He masked his surprise with a sigh of relief. "I sure do, Nellie. I decided to start with the shipping department in my survey of the company. I'm hoping to come up with some ideas on how to increase the efficiency of moving the product. By the way, how is Nick doing this morning?" he asked, deliberately shifting the subject.

"I think he's going to be okay. They won't tell you much over the phone. I came in early so I could take care of a couple of things Nick was concerned about. I'll make a run out to the hospital a little later."

"Good idea. Listen, my stuff can wait. I think I've picked up a general idea of how the department works. When Nick comes back and has some free time, he can sort things out for me. I'm betting there're some headaches he'd like to get rid of, and I want to be of help if I can.''

She simply nodded and then watched him as he made his way across the open area to the elevator. He couldn't tell if Nellie had bought the bag of lies.

The rest of the day hadn't produced anything of immediate interest. He'd spent time making himself visible and chatting with various staff. The hours he spent on Arthur's computer didn't reveal any hint of what might have been there once and since erased.

Della pointedly ignored him, and by the time four o'clock came, he felt like a swimmer who'd been battling his way upstream. He needed something to renew his energy. The truth surprised him—he needed Carolyn's company.

When he arrived at the mansion, he saw Lisa's car in the garage. Letting himself into the house, he headed up the stairs to see if Carolyn was in their suite.

The outer sitting room was empty and so was the bedroom, but when he peeked into the study, his breath caught. He couldn't believe his eyes.

''Oh, hi,'' she said, turning away from a bookcase and walking toward him. ''I was looking for something to read.''

He saw her mouth move, but the words didn't register. The lines and curves of her body in the clinging red dress assaulted his senses. He just stared at her. If they'd been in the bedroom, he wasn't sure what would have happened. She looked so damn alluring, tantalizing and seductive that his body instantly reacted with a hot need to claim her.

He silently swore. He couldn't take this kind of temptation. He'd been forcing himself to honor his commitment to her, and it was getting more difficult all the time. He sure as hell didn't need any more enticements to push him into breaking his promise.

"Don't you like my new look?" she asked in an anxious tone as he just stood there, gaping at her.

"It's...it's..." He searched for the right word and finally gave up. "No, I don't. It isn't you."

"Really? And what is me, exactly?" she asked testily. "Last year's fashion? Is that what you're saying?"

He tried to recover from his faux pas. "I'm saying you don't have to parade your...assets in clothes like that. It gives the wrong impression."

"Are you talking from a detached perspective or a personal one?" she challenged as she slowly walked toward him.

He knew if he touched her, no amount of resolve was going to keep him from kissing her. She'd been engaging his feelings to the deepest levels from the beginning, but he'd been able to keep his desire in check because she hadn't played into the growing attraction between them.

When she stopped in front of him, he thought she was going to challenge his fortitude with some sexy move. Instead, she gave him a wan smile.

"You're right, of course. Don't worry, Adam. This was an experiment, and Lisa was wrong."

"Wrong about what?"

"She said my husband would take one look at me and carry me off to bed. I guess, maybe, I was foolishly dreaming something like that might happen— if things were different."

He looked into her clear blue eyes. "If things were different, something would have happened before now. You don't need a dress like that to get my attention.''

He made the mistake of cupping her chin with his hand, and she made only the slightest movement toward him, but it was enough. He bent his head, and kissed her gently, a surge of desire humming through him. Her lips were soft and sweet, and he silently groaned as his mouth played on hers. As her arms crept up around his neck to deepen the kiss, he finally came to himself and gently set her away from him.

He had no business playing with her emotions at a time when she was trying to find herself. She was a millionaire, and once she was able to enjoy all the privileges that went with wealth, the world would bow at her feet. Any interest she had in him would quickly disappear. Neither spoke as they searched the other's face.

"I'm sorry, Carolyn," he finally murmured. "I didn't mean for that to happen." He grinned sheepishly. "It must be that darn dress."

"Doesn't Angel wear sexy clothes?" she asked pointedly.

"Who?" What in hell...?

"Angel. The woman you call Angel. Please don't deny it."

Shaken by his kiss and reeling with desire, Carolyn felt all her apprehension and anxiety come pouring out. It was almost as if some jealous little devil was sitting on her shoulder, prodding her. "Why couldn't you be honest with me, Adam?"

"It's not what think, Carolyn. You've jumped to the wrong conclusion."

"I may have jumped to a lot of wrong conclusions," she answered shortly. "As far as I know, you could have been feeding me nothing but lies from the moment we met. I should have taken time to investigate, but you kept saying we couldn't waste any time. Insisting we get legally married could have been a very clever move on your part. How do I know I'm not the victim of a horrendous money scam you and Bancroft cooked up?"

He started to answer and then held up his hand for silence. Quickly he crossed the room to the door to the hall and jerked it open.

He peered out. The hall was empty. Several doors along the corridor stood open. He couldn't be sure if anyone had had time to duck out of sight. Undoubtedly there was also a servants' stairway in this wing of the house. Maybe his intuition was all wrong. It was probably the loudness of Carolyn's voice that had triggered his apprehension.

He closed the door and returned to Carolyn, standing there with her eyes still snapping. He couldn't believe that a remark about a sexy dress and his calls to his superior had released a flood of unfounded suspicion. Did she really believe he might be setting her up to get his hands on her inheritance? Was this what she'd been thinking all along? And here he'd been so pleased at how harmoniously they'd been working together. He must have dropped the ball without knowing it.

"I can explain all this, Carolyn."

"Please do," she invited coolly.

He hesitated, knowing he couldn't identify his superior, Angelica Rivers, for his own protection and hers. It was one of the cardinal rules of the agency not to establish a trail that someone might follow from an undercover agent to another person.

"I don't know how much you overheard," he began hesitantly, trying to use an effective interrogation tool to find out what the person knows.

"I didn't hear very much. And I wasn't eavesdropping," she hastened to assure him. "I simply heard you on the phone, calling someone Angel. I also know that you've been making calls after you thought I was asleep, and the whole thing suggests flagrant dishonesty about what you've told me." She searched his face. "I can't help asking myself why you would lie to me about not having any romantic attachments, unless it ties in with other lies you've told me. Lies that could make a total fool out of me."

"I haven't told you any lies about my private life or about this situation at Horizon," he countered firmly. He wanted to tell her that no woman had even come close to touching his heart since he'd lost Marietta. Not until now. Didn't she realize how just being around her had made him aware of the emptiness in his life? Sometimes his outward expression of tender caring came from deep within his very being. There was little pretense in the endearments he spoke for other ears, and the kiss he'd given her had vibrated through every cell in his body. How could she question his sincerity and integrity?

"Please believe me, Carolyn. I've been totally honest with you. You should have mentioned this whole 'Angel' thing before it festered. I assure you that my calls have not been made to a sweetheart or mistress. More than that, I cannot say until this investigation is over."

She blinked, as if she couldn't believe he was finished explaining. "That's it?"

"Either you accept the truth of what I'm telling you or you don't," he said flatly. He knew better than to think he could bend her to his will if she set her mind against it. "My motivation is still the same. I just want to stop the pain and death of innocent people as quickly as I can. If you don't believe that's what all this is about, I can't force you to continue. It's a dangerous game. Are you still in, or are you out?"

Without answering, she crossed to the couch and sat down. Leaning forward, she rested her head in her hands as if her thoughts were too heavy. She looked so fragile and vulnerable that he had to fight his impulse to go and cuddle her.

When she finally raised her head, his heart caught in his throat. "I'm still in," she said.

Because his chest was too tight to express his feelings of relief, he said casually, as if nothing more important was on his mind, "Morna is expecting us for dinner. Maybe we should be on time tonight."

She nodded and walked past him as if they were two strangers who had somehow ended up together on a fast train to emotional disaster.

Chapter Ten

Dinner was a dismal affair. Buddy was the only one who showed any sign of good humor. He'd been fishing with a friend and bragged about the catch they'd made as if everyone at the table was interested in every detail. Ignoring his mother's frown, he kept motioning for Seika to fill his wineglass.

Carolyn decided that Della and Lisa must have had a mother-daughter confrontation just before dinner, because they weren't speaking to each other. Jasper didn't seem to notice anything that was going on at the table. He gave his attention to his meal and his only comment was, "The salmon seems a bit dry."

Adam asked Della some questions about how her day went, but only received polite, vague answers. He played the devoted husband, smiling at Carolyn and asking her if she wanted more rolls and rice pilaf, even though it should have been obvious to him that she was only picking at her food.

Every time he brushed her arm, she tensed. The memory of his mouth seductively capturing hers lingered with poignant intensity. She was aware of his long legs inches from hers under the table, felt the magnetic draw his nearness exerted.

The verbal confrontation they'd had after the kiss only seemed to heighten the bewildering fact that she was falling in love with him. Even though he might be telling the truth about not having any romantic attachments, he had his own agenda. For the moment she was a necessary ingredient in that agenda, but that would change. And then what? He'd be on his way to a new assignment. Once again she was leaving herself open to hurt and abandonment.

When the excruciatingly long meal was over, Jasper surprised Carolyn by solemnly asking her to accompany him into the library. "I have something to show you."

His invitation didn't include Adam, but Carolyn was grateful that he acted as if it did. He gave her a wink and a smile as he placed a hand on her arm, then guided her out of the dining room and along a spacious hallway behind Jasper's lean figure. When Jasper turned into a large room filled with bookcases and comfortable leather furniture, they followed.

What was Jasper's intention? she wondered. Was he going to reveal some devastating truth about her parentage?

Carolyn had made inquiries about pictures and information about her mother, but without success. She had never quite believed that both her mother's father and brother could be completely in the dark about who had gotten her pregnant. Had she been raped by some stranger? Had some lowlife preyed on her innocence?

"It's okay," Adam reassured her quietly as if

reading her thoughts. "Remember, whatever you learn about your parentage doesn't change who you are. You've already proved your stature as a very lovely, intelligent, caring human being."

She gave him a grateful smile as Jasper motioned for them to sit on a deep leather couch. He cleared his throat and made a big production of handing Carolyn an envelope containing old photos.

"Most of them are of me," Jasper confessed. "But your mother's in some."

Carolyn's hands trembled slightly as she looked at the snapshots. Jasper was the main subject of all of the photos. He was a young man in his late teens, and a child of eight or nine was either smiling or making faces in the background. *My mother?* Carolyn let the tip of one finger trace her mother's pretty features, and the grin on her face. She appeared to be a happy child. What had gone wrong? Why had Alicia run away from home? And left a child unnamed and unwanted?

"And you don't have any pictures of her mother when she was older?" Adam asked, unable to believe that these few snapshots were all there were.

Jasper frowned. "I don't know what happened to the box of photographs that used to be in the library. When Della moved in, she cleaned out a whole lot of old stuff that had been lying around gathering dust. Of course, we didn't know then what was going to happen. I mean, who would have thought that Alicia's daughter would appear out of nowhere? It does seem unbelievable, doesn't it?"

"Yes, it does," Carolyn agreed. "I wonder what my mother would say about all this? Do you think she might be as surprised as anyone that her father left his fortune to her daughter?''

Jasper declined to speculate and just shrugged his bony shoulders. Carolyn handed back the photos and he didn't offer to let her keep them. He just tossed them into a desk drawer as if they were of little value.

Adam studied Jasper. There was no softness in the blue of the man's eyes as he looked at Carolyn, and the unfeeling expression verified what Adam had suspected all along. The man was not the detached, vague personality that he pretended to be. A deep rancor seemed to be simmering beneath Jasper's exterior of a single-minded scientist. Adam wondered how much responsibility he bore for his sister's unhappy life. More importantly, Adam was concerned that now Carolyn might have become the focus of that bitterness and resentment.

Carolyn thanked her uncle politely for sharing the photos. When they left the library, she and Adam made their way to their wing of the house. She pretended a desire for an early night, and only nodded when Adam said he was going to take a little walk before turning in.

The night air was heavy as he let himself out a side door on the ground floor. Strolling on a path around the perimeter of the house, he was conscious of the building's enormity. The Stanford mansion was in the same class as the Vanderbilt or Astor estates. Carolyn's inheritance had vaulted her into a position that would ensure she'd marry wealth, a man of social prestige.

Adam scowled and kicked a small stone out of the way. A quiver of jealousy surprised him, and he had to remind himself that his challenge was to bring her safely through this investigation and bless her future happiness. As he looked up at the second-floor windows, he saw that lights were on in Della's home office and was tempted to drop in on her for a casual chat. He knew that such a visit would be completely out of context with his undercover role; Adam knew better than to attract any kind of attention that could sabotage the whole investigation. Why would a new bridegroom be wandering around the house alone, instead of curled up in bed with his beautiful new wife?

As he returned to the house, uppermost in his mind was the need to mend fences with Carolyn as quickly as possible. It was imperative that they keep the pretense intact. Fortunately everyone at dinner seemed to be too involved with their own thoughts to notice the strain between them. At least he hoped that was the case—you never knew how much a single look or a tone of voice could give away. If Carolyn was still awake when he got back to their room, they'd better have another talk.

He was disappointed to find her in bed and apparently asleep, though he couldn't be sure she wasn't feigning sleep to avoid him. He sighed. First thing tomorrow, before they went down to breakfast, they'd have to set things straight between them.

AT TWO IN THE MORNING, Carolyn awoke screaming from a recurring childhood nightmare that had come back with a vengeance. The dream had initially started after a malicious older orphan had taunted Carolyn, saying she'd been found behind a stack of wood at the foundling home. The cruel girl had even taken Carolyn out to show her the place where the logs were stacked. In her nightmare Carolyn was buried under the heavy wood, and no matter how frantically she cried and struggled to get free, someone was about to set fire to the wood logs covering her.

Her screams instantly woke Adam, and as he reached for her across the bed, she flayed at him and kept crying.

"Don't burn me. Don't burn me." She fought him with the fierceness of a trapped animal. Her nails scratched his arms as he tried to soothe her.

"Carolyn, wake up. You're okay. You're okay."

Slowly his voice penetrated the haze in her mind, and staring at him, wide-eyed, she began to climb out of the swirling fear that had engulfed her.

"You were dreaming. You're all right."

Her breath was coming in gulps, and she could still feel the imaginary flames and the heavy weight of the wood on her. He put his arms around her and gradually she let her body slump against his.

He stroked her hair as he touched his lips to her tear-streaked cheek, then he gathered her close.

In the circle of his protective arms, the terror still racing through her body began to ease. After a few minutes the drumming of her heart slowed, and her breathing deepened. She closed her eyes and let the warmth of his body act as a barricade to the horror of the nightmare.

"You okay?" he asked gently, and she nodded as they lay quietly together. The only sound was the muted hum of the bedside clock. As he held her in his arms, Adam was acutely aware of the length of her body pressed against his. Even the nightclothes they both wore were little defense against his thoughts of what her tantalizing nakedness would be like. He ached to run his hands over her tempting curves and bring his lips to her trembling mouth.

With great effort, he pulled his thoughts away from this dangerous avenue of thinking. In her dazed and vulnerable state, she would probably respond. And then what? Would she ever believe that he had truly intended to keep their marriage a platonic one? Once they made love, there would be no going back, and neither of them needed to be emotionally torn apart when the stakes were so high.

He wasn't surprised when she slowly removed herself from his embrace and lay on her back, looking up at the ceiling.

"Do you want to tell me about it?" he asked gently, raising himself on one elbow, and looking down at her. "Maybe it would help."

"I'm...I'm sorry," she stammered. She hadn't had the nightmare for a long time and she was embarrassed by her hysterics. What must he think of her? She'd been chastised and ridiculed by foster parents for disturbing the whole house with her "childish tantrums."

"There's nothing to be sorry about," he assured her as he gently turned her face toward him. One of the window drapes had not been drawn fully closed, letting moonlight into the room. Slivers of light were reflected in her moist eyes, making them lovelier than ever, but he was aware of the pain in their depths. "There's no crime in having a bad dream, sweet Carolyn."

She searched his face as if seeking reassurance. Then she moistened her lips and told him the story.

By the time she'd finished, such anger had built up in him that he wanted to punish someone for the anguish she'd suffered. If he'd had any doubts that she deserved the good fortune that had come her way, they were swept away. He vowed then and there that if anyone ever hurt her again, they'd have to answer to him.

"I'm glad you told me," he said as he tucked her, almost like a child, in the crook of his arm. She didn't resist or pull away, but closed her eyes and took a deep breath as if just the telling had restored her.

When her measured breathing told him she'd fallen asleep, he eased back to his side of the bed. He couldn't depend on his willpower to control the temptation he'd feel if he awoke and found her warm, inviting body next to his. It had been far too long since he'd been sexually satisfied. He knew damn well that he'd found a woman who could fire a passion that had been dormant since Marietta's death. He also knew that he was in danger of falling in love with a woman who would only bring him another heartache. He silently groaned. Why couldn't Arthur Stanford's long-lost granddaughter been someone less beautiful and captivating? The assignment was difficult enough. He sure as hell didn't need his heart put through the wringer at the same time.

CAROLYN OVERSLEPT THE next morning and awoke with a start when Adam entered the room with a breakfast tray.

"Hi, sweetness."

She was startled at the endearment. There was no

one around to hear it. Was he feeling sorry for her because of the nightmare? Her pride instantly began to prickle and she sat up. She couldn't stand to be pitied. "What's all this?"

"I thought you deserved breakfast in bed. Especially when the atmosphere in the breakfast room seems to be a repeat of last night's dinner. Of course, if you'd rather face Jasper's glower and Della's caustic remarks, I can take the tray back."

"Not on your life." She fluffed the pillow behind her and sat up straighter. He put the tray on her lap. Sniffing and lifting the lids, she saw cereal, biscuits and strawberries with cream. Relaxing, she quipped, "Thank you, sir. You're a good man."

You don't know how good, he thought wryly. She'd never know how utterly desirable she'd been lying in his arms. He deserved a medal for exemplary behavior.

"What are your plans for the day?" he asked as he lowered himself on a corner of the bed.

She looked thoughtful as she bit into a biscuit. "I don't really know. Any suggestions?"

"I thought we might go shopping for a car. It seems to me you should have wheels of your own. And…"

"And what?" she prodded when he hesitated.

"I'd feel better about you driving yourself around, instead of depending on someone."

She searched his face. "Is there something you're not telling me? Nothing happened yesterday when Lisa was chauffeuring us around. And I can always drive one of the cars in the garage."

"It's just better to control as many variables as we can."

"I don't know what that means," she admitted, frowning.

"It means that it's easier to make sure one car is safe than two or three."

"Safe?" she echoed, knowing exactly what he meant. He wasn't talking about ordinary mechanical problems. "You don't think…" Her voice trailed off.

"I'm not thinking anything definite at the moment, but you need a car and I think it's a good idea to get one now. How about it? What kind of car have you always wanted?"

"One that has good tires and always starts on the first try."

He laughed. "I think we can find one like that."

CAROLYN COULDN'T DECIDE which of her new clothes to wear. Should she save them for a special occasion? *Like buying your first new car?* an inner voice asked. She finally chose a pair of light-wool maroon pants that hugged her slender hips, and a lavender cotton blouse, then accented the outfit with a bold gold-and-amethyst necklace. She pulled her hair high on her head to show off matching earrings and dabbed sinfully expensive perfume behind her ears.

Adam whistled when he saw her. "You look like a lady whose ready to buy the fanciest car on wheels. Let's go make some salesman's day."

Finding the right car didn't turn out to be as easy as Adam had thought. Carolyn was completely blown away by the fact that she could write out a check for any new-model automobile that struck her fancy. She wandered through showrooms like a child offered so many sweets it's impossible to make a choice.

"How about this one?"

"Do you want something bigger?"

"This blue one matches your eyes," he said, as they viewed a snappy little sports car.

"I don't think that's me," she said cautiously. "Maybe something a little bigger and not so showy."

She finally decided on a midsize foreign model, white with a burgundy interior. Adam breathed a sigh of relief.

The dealership agreed to deliver it to the house that afternoon. They grabbed a quick lunch and Adam drove them in his rental to Horizon.

As he parked he said, "I think I should spend some time in the business office." Quickly he told her about his breakfast chat with Susan Kimble. "She intrigues me. I learned from someone else that she's the business manager. That's a position of great responsibility."

"You don't think she has anything to do with the black-market drugs, do you?" Carolyn looked at him in surprise. "She seems so...so nice."

"At this early stage I'm simply looking for a thread I can unravel. Then I'll follow it and see where it leads. The closer we get to identifying the guilty ones, the more likely they'll try to stop us. Once that happens, the danger increases. Your position alone, Carolyn, puts you in jeopardy," he warned her. "Don't do anything on your own without checking with me first."

Carolyn's first impulse—to remind him that she could take care of herself—died when she saw the hard glint in his eyes. His professional briskness didn't invite any argument, and there was a fierceness about him that startled her. Was this the same man who'd held her tenderly last night and soothed her fears? It was ironic that she wore his wedding ring and slept every night in the same bed with him. She really didn't know Adam Lawrence at all.

"All right, I won't, but I don't like the idea of tagging around after you all day."

His expression softened. This flare of independence was one of the things he loved about her. She wanted to be her own person no matter the circumstances, and he wouldn't want to force her into a role that would crush that. At the same time, he intended to keep a tight rein on her activities.

"Why don't you spend the day with Della?" he suggested. "After all, if I weren't in the picture, that's what you'd naturally be doing to get a feel for the company."

"She probably thinks I'm some kind of a dimwit, spending my time shopping with Lisa and sleeping late in the mornings," Carolyn lamented.

Adam grinned. "Exactly. By now Della's anxiety about your taking over should have worn off. Her defenses will be down, and no telling what you'll be able to learn."

"I don't even know what I should be looking for. None of this is in my area of expertise," she reminded him. How could he expect her to function as his trained investigative partner?

"For the moment just be aware of the way Della relates to different people. If you pick up any inconsistencies, make a mental note of them."

"Inconsistencies like what?"

"Relating to someone in a way that is outside normal work interaction. Whoever is orchestrating this black-market fraud within the company isn't doing it alone. It's too big of an operation and too complicated."

If the evidence against Horizon hadn't been so conclusive, she would have argued that the company was innocent of any wrongdoing. More than anything she wished that Adam was wrong, but there was no discounting his conviction and determination. He'd lost someone he loved, and others would die if they didn't bring the guilty ones to justice.

She firmed her chin. "All right. I'll do my best. I've depended on my intuition about people more than once."

They entered the building together, and for the benefit of any peering eyes, he gave her a hug and said, "See you in a while, darling."

He blew her a kiss as he took the elevator up to the second floor, and Carolyn was smiling when she reached Della's office. She warmly greeted the secretary sitting at an outer desk.

"Hello, I'm Carolyn Lawrence. Is Mrs. Denison in?"

"I'm sure she will be for you, Mrs. Lawrence. Just a moment and I'll buzz her."

Della must have already been on her feet when she heard who was waiting to see her, for her door jerked open only a second later. "For heaven's sake, Carolyn, you don't need to be announced. Why didn't you use the connecting door between the offices?"

"I haven't been to my office yet," Carolyn confessed. "I've been out buying a car." She knew she was deliberately fostering the impression that Adam wanted Della to have of her. Pleasure-seeking. Unmotivated. Dragging her feet about assuming any responsibility in the company.

"Well, come in. I was just having a little conference with Cliff, but we're almost through."

Carolyn's sense of well-being instantly dissipated as Cliff rose from a chair in front of Della's desk and gave her that knowing smile of his. "Good afternoon, Caro. Did I hear you say you've bought yourself a car?" He winked. "A Cadillac, no doubt, complete with all the bells and whistles."

"Sorry to disappoint you, Cliff," she replied without elaborating. It wasn't any of his damn business what kind of car she bought. Turning to Della, she smiled apologetically. "Sorry to interrupt. If you don't mind, I'll just sit quietly while you take care of business."

"Of course." Della motioned to a leather chair in the conversational grouping of furniture that was some distance from her desk and where Cliff sat. Then she took some papers from her desk and leaning over his shoulder, talked quietly to him.

Their voices were muffled, and Carolyn had no idea if they were talking about the papers or about something else. When the intercom buzzed, Della listened and then said to Cliff, "Excuse me a minute. I have to confer with my secretary."

She left the office, it was obvious to Carolyn that whatever Della needed to say to her secretary, she didn't want to be overheard. Cliff got up from his chair and sauntered over to where Carolyn was sitting.

"How's the pretty little rich girl doing?" he

asked in that affable way of his. Only the glint in his eye told her there was a hidden agenda in his question.

"The same as always," she answered pointedly. "Nothing's changed really. I guess I could wake up tomorrow and go back to my old life, if that's the way things turned out."

"That would be a real shame. I'd sure hate to see you dragging a lot of old baggage around."

"What makes you think I am? I assure you that I cut myself loose from my past mistakes a long time ago. How about you, Cliff?"

The question was a subtle way of reminding him that blackmail could work both ways. She knew things about him he wouldn't want spread around, and as far as she was concerned he had a lot more to lose than she did. Then a thought like electricity shot through her.

Maybe Cliff wasn't thinking of blackmailing her for money, but for her silence! If he was connected with the black-market trade, he would use everything he could to keep her from blowing the whistle.

"I never was one for compromise, Cliff," she warned him.

"That's too bad, Caro." He started to say something more, but Della returned to her office, and his mask fell back in place. He left the office a few minutes later.

The rest of the afternoon Carolyn observed Della working at the computer, talking on the phone to people Carolyn didn't know and solving problems she didn't bother to explain to Carolyn. Carolyn realized that if she was to get a handle on the finances of the company, she was going to have to spend time looking over Della's records. With her background, she'd be able to see for herself if the company was solvent. It was a little disturbing to realize how this one woman controlled so many areas. Carolyn couldn't help but wonder if her grandfather had placed blind trust in Della Denison.

When Adam was ready to leave the business office, it was quitting time. His time with Susan had been about as productive as Carolyn's. He'd observed the mechanics, but Susan hadn't been very forthcoming about the details of the operation. Certainly he hadn't been able to pick up any hints how false orders could be sent through the system.

They decided against going back to the mansion for dinner. Enduring another family dinner like the one the night before held no attraction. When Carolyn informed Della they'd be eating out, much to their surprise, she recommended a steak-and-lobster restaurant located in a small shopping area north of the city.

The drive along the waterfront was pleasant, and the food turned out to be everything Della had claimed. As Carolyn and Adam relaxed and enjoyed their meal, they deliberately avoided any stressful topic of conversation.

For a couple of hours they were just two people getting to know each other. After dinner they strolled along a pedestrian walkway lined with inviting stores.

"You could go inside and buy anything that strikes your fancy," Adam reminded her.

"I've never been into stuff-ology," she admitted. "I don't have to own things to enjoy them."

He grinned. "Somehow I don't think that's going

to change. But now you can buy gifts for other people. How about your friend Rosie?''

Carolyn's eyes sparkled. ''Wonderful idea. I'm going to buy her a music box. She used to drive me crazy listening to every one displayed in a store, knowing full well she couldn't afford to buy any of them.''

They found a gift store, and Carolyn chose a miniature carousel with tiny pastel horses. Delighted with her gift, she slipped her arm through Adam's as they retraced their steps to their car.

''How about going for a drive?'' he asked as if the two of them were on a date. ''It's a lovely clear night. We might even park and count the stars.''

''Are your intentions honorable?'' she asked with mock solemnity. He looked devastatingly handsome and sexy in his matching beige chambray shirt and trousers.

''Absolutely.''

''It's a beautiful night,'' she said. ''Maybe we shouldn't waste it.'' She was surprised at her boldness. Flirting had never been part of her repertoire, and she felt a little nervous. What would she do if he thought she was coming on to him in a sexual way? Making out in a car when they had a huge bed waiting for them seemed utterly ridiculous.

They drove south for a few miles, and then Adam turned onto a small road leading to an elevated viewpoint area overlooking Puget Sound. Another car was parked there, but it left almost immediately.

A beach stretched at the bottom of a steep, rocky incline. As Adam turned off the ignition, Carolyn said, ''I love the sound of the surf. Do you think there's a way to climb down to the water?''

"Looks too steep, but we can check it out."

They were walking hand in hand toward the edge of the parking area when it happened.

The sound of an engine roar behind them sent a warning. They swung around and saw a car was coming straight at them.

Blinded by the headlights, Carolyn screamed. Her legs wouldn't work. Paralyzed, she stiffened against the impending impact.

At the last second Adam gave her a vicious shove.

Screaming brakes sounded in their ears as they tumbled head over heels down the rocky embankment to the water's edge.

Chapter Eleven

Carolyn landed on her back in the cold, wet sand. Stunned, she saw the stars in the sky whirling like an off balance top. Everything had happened so fast that for one incoherent moment she thought she must be dreaming, but her bruised body assured her she was fully conscious.

When she heard Adam groan, all doubts faded. Gasping for breath, she pushed herself into a sitting position. Every inch of her battered body ached. Gingerly she moved her legs to make sure that nothing was broken, and then her frantic gaze swept the narrow, rock-littered strip of sand. The sound of the surf muffled the direction Adam's groans were coming from, and she couldn't see him.

"Adam! Where are you?" No sign of him on the narrow strip of sand as she got unsteadily to her feet. He must have been caught in the rocks and not fallen all the way down to the water's edge.

"Adam!" Brushing strands of sandy hair away from her face, she searched the rocky incline. At first she didn't see anything in the light-and-dark pattern of tumbled rocks, but as her anxious eyes continued to scan the slope, she saw a slight movement.

Heedless of her bruises, she clamored upward. She heard his groans before she reached him. He was lying between two boulders that had stopped his downward plunge, and one of them had been dislodged and was lying right on top of him. His groans were efforts to get the large rock off him.

Between the two of them, they were able to move it and send it tumbling down the slope to the water below. Bending over him, she ordered in a tone that brooked no argument, "Don't move."

She checked his pulse. Its steady rhythm was reassuring. Her hands moved quickly over his hips, legs, arms and head. No outward signs of injury.

"What hurts?"

"What doesn't?" he answered as he sat up, then assured her he was all right. She let out a sigh of relief. No broken ribs.

He asked anxiously, "What about you?"

"Oh, I made it all the way to the bottom and landed on some soft sand. Piece of cake," she lied, trying not to wince every time she moved. She looked upward and silently groaned.

"Do you want to wait awhile before we climb back up to the car?"

She shook her head. Strained muscles only tightened up as time passed. She hated to think what their bruised bodies would feel like in the morning.

Her voice was rather shaky as she asked, "Do you think it's safe?"

He knew what she was asking. *Did he think someone stuck around, waiting to finish the job?* The sound of screeching brakes still echoed in his ears. Obviously the plan had been to run them over with a car, and Adam doubted that the assailant had stuck around, because anyone with a gun could have picked them off already.

"Yes, I think it's safe," he said, and prayed to God he was right.

The climb up the rocky slope wasn't as excruciating as either of them feared. It was a miracle they'd come out of the ordeal with only scratches and bruises.

When they reached the top of the incline, Adam stood protectively in front of Carolyn as he surveyed the parking area.

Empty except for their car.

He listened for any hint of an idling engine, but only faint night sounds and the hum of distant traffic met his ears.

"Okay, let's do it." He nodded to Carolyn and they ran across the open space to the safety of their car. As soon as they were inside, Adam started the engine, turned the car around and headed back toward the center of the city.

Carolyn just sat there in a kind of blessed shock. It had all happened so fast she was still trying to collect her thoughts and emotions.

"Did you have any glimpse of the car at all?" Adam asked.

She shook her head. "There wasn't time."

"Those damn headlights blinded us the minute we turned around. The only thing I'm sure of is that it was a car, not a van or truck."

"We have to tell the police," Carolyn said. She hated the thought of being in the public eye, but what choice did they have? Someone had tried to kill them.

"No," Adam said. "We don't want to bring the local law enforcement into this."

"But—" Carolyn started to protest.

"The local authorities could blow our cover. Division of authority results in chaos most of the time, and there's no way to bring local law enforcement into this without complicating our federal investigation at Horizon. My boss would have my head if I invited that kind of a leak about my undercover status."

"But how can we keep quiet about this?" Her voice rose. "We can't just ignore it."

"I have no intention of ignoring it," he answered patiently. "When something like this happens, it's a warning signal. We've got to move faster." He gave her a searching look. "You said nothing happened with Della this afternoon."

She nodded. "I didn't see or hear anything amiss." Then she swallowed. "I did have a little confrontation with Cliff, though. Nothing about the company," she added hastily. "It was personal."

One of Adam's hands tapped the steering wheel impatiently. "Dammit, Carolyn, you've got to tell me everything. I don't care if it's personal or not."

Feeling contrite, Carolyn repeated the conversation with Cliff. "He knows I'm not going to pay him a cent."

"Let me get this straight. You told him in so many words that you wouldn't be above using his past to discredit him?"

"I guess what I really told him was that two could play that game."

He groaned. "You don't even know the name of the game, my sweet Carolyn."

"You don't think...? No, Cliff wouldn't do something like this," she insisted. "The guy's a manipulator, a con artist, but he's not a murderer. Besides, Della suggested the restaurant. She knew we were going to be there and could have followed after dinner."

"Or she could have mentioned the fact to who knows how many other people. If we remain quiet about this, we may catch someone lying about not knowing where we had dinner."

"And how are we going to explain looking like two castaways?"

"We'll go in the side door of the house that leads up to our suite on the second floor. With luck, we can slip in and out whenever we want, without anyone seeing us."

Carolyn leaned her head back against the seat. At the moment she was too sore and tired to play detective. All she wanted was a nice hot bath, and something dry and clean to put on.

They saw her new white car in the garage as they pulled in, but the place was noticeably empty of any of the cars that the rest of the household used. Lisa and Buddy were usually late getting home, so it was no surprise that their cars weren't there, but it was unusual for Della and Jasper to be out after dinner.

Adam made a mental note to try to learn their whereabouts for the evening. He and Carolyn made it up to their suite without seeing anyone. After quietly closing the door, they turned on the light, and for the first time, got a good look at themselves.

Their clothes were dirty and torn, their arms and legs scratched and bruised. They looked like refugees from some war. If the circumstances hadn't been so dire, they might have had a good laugh at themselves.

"You can shower first," Carolyn said.

"Or we could share," he offered with an innocent lift of his eyebrows.

"We could," she answered thoughtfully as if giving the idea serious consideration. "But I'm holding out for a long, leisurely bath—alone."

"Well, you can't blame a guy for trying."

While he was in the bathroom, she stripped and then checked herself for cuts and scrapes. Then she took some sterile pads out of her doctor's kit and cleaned them. She'd just slipped into a flowing caftan that Lisa had persuaded her to buy when Adam came out of the bathroom.

"It's all yours." He had a towel wrapped around his waist. A deep scratch ran down one leg, and a large, ugly bruise on one shoulder. His arms were badly scratched.

She took one look at him and handed him the bottle of antiseptic and sterile pads. "Make sure you clean them thoroughly."

"Wait a minute. Having a doctor in the house should guarantee a little extra attention. I can wait until you're finished with your bath," he offered.

"I'm very sorry, sir, but I don't make house calls." She gave his towel a saucy pull and then turned away quickly, ignoring the temptation to give him a rather extensive physical right then and there.

NEITHER OF THEM SLEPT worth a darn that night. Stiff and sore, Adam wasn't even tempted to do any harmless cuddling. He could hear Carolyn groan as she turned over, and he knew her lovely body had been battered as much as his.

As he lay there, he tried to tie the incident to any of the facts they already had. Someone had tried to run them down. This convinced Adam more than ever that Arthur Stanford's death was not an accident. It was obvious that the murderer was using the same method of operation, and it was imperative to catch him before he killed again. Someone was getting nervous. Who? Adam went over the possible suspects and came up empty.

When he moved to get out of bed, Carolyn's eyelids lifted slowly and she mumbled, "Tell me it's not time to get up."

"Sorry, I never lie. Well, almost never." He grinned as he stood by the bed in his striped pajama bottoms looking down at her. "I don't suppose you'd believe me if I told you that you look ravishing this morning, Mrs. Lawrence."

"Are you asking for another bruise?"

"No, thank you. I'll settle for the ones I have."

"You don't look too bad, considering," she offered, squinting at him.

"I guess 'not too bad' will have to do."

"You'll need to wear long sleeves and a button-up shirt. You must have used your arms to cover your face when you fell. Luckily there are no telltale marks there." She touched her own face. "How about me? Did any bruises show up during the night?"

He sat down on the edge of the bed, and lightly cupping her chin, he slowly turned her face one direction and then the other.

"Hmm, I'm not sure."

Before she could put up a hand in protest, he bent his head and trailed his lips from her forehead to the corner of her mouth, and the warm curve of her neck.

She was about to give in to the invitation to put her arms around his neck, but as she raised her arms, she winced, and when she touched the bruise on his shoulder he grimaced. She couldn't control a giggle, and they both started laughing.

"Sad shape we're in."

Their shared laughter kept at bay the stark reality of the night before and the tragedy it might have been.

"I prescribe a day of R and R," she told him, knowing full well that it was only wishful thinking. "After all, today *is* Sunday."

"A good day to snoop around when Horizon is virtually empty," he answered readily. "Let's go down to breakfast and see what the rest of the household has planned for the day."

She would have preferred to stay holed up in their suite and nurse back her fragile courage, but she knew it wouldn't do any good to argue. She wasn't ready to face anyone who might have been the one behind the wheel of that car. How could she pretend that nothing had happened?

They dressed carefully in clothes that covered their cuts and bruises. Adam put on blue slacks and a long-sleeve pullover with a narrow turtleneck collar. He nodded his approval of Carolyn's new jeans and matching denim shirt. All evidence of their injuries were nicely covered as they went downstairs for breakfast.

They could smell coffee and cooking odors coming from the kitchen, but the table in the morning room had not been set yet. Apparently breakfast was scheduled late on Sunday.

"Do we dare?" Carolyn asked, hesitating at a closed door that led into the kitchen.

"It's your house and your kitchen," Adam gently reminded her, adding with a grin, "I'll be right behind to catch you if you get thrown out."

To their surprise there were already four people in the kitchen. Mr. Lei and his older daughter, Lotuse, were busy at one end of the kitchen. Seika was packing a lunch, and Buddy was sitting at the kitchen table, watching her.

"Be sure and put in plenty of those nut cookies you like, Seika," he told her. "We'll be gone all day, you know. There's nothing in the galley to eat and—" He broke off as Carolyn and Adam came into the room. "Well, good morning. Are you folks heading out somewhere early, too?"

Before either of them could answer, Seika hurried over to Carolyn anxiously. "It's okay I go? Day off today, yes?"

"I...I don't know," Carolyn stammered.

"If Morna gave you a day off, Seika, I'm sure no one else is going to object," Buddy said, jumping in. "We're going to take a little run up to Victoria. Would you two like to join us? Too bad I don't have a bigger boat—we could really make an overnight party of it if I did." He winked at Carolyn. "If you get into boating, maybe we could get one of those fancy new cruisers."

"Maybe," she said. First Lisa and now Buddy, willing and ready to help her spend money. The two of them obviously enjoyed the good things in life, but Carolyn couldn't help but wonder if Della's children's insatiable appetites for spending had caused their mother to look for illegal means to supplant her income.

"What do Della and Jasper usually do on Sunday?" Adam asked, wanting to make sure the coast was clear to take a closer look inside the company.

He shrugged. "Not much. I guess they drove up to their place in the mountains last night. They'll spend the day and come back before dinner tonight. Bor-or-ing. We have better things to do, don't we, Seika?" He gave her a look that brought a blush to her pretty face.

Carolyn shot a glance at the girl's father, who was still giving his attention to preparing a roast for the oven. Carolyn was certain he could overhear their conversation, but he didn't seem to be concerned that the young man in the house was having a romantic relationship with his daughter. Lotuse, on the other hand, scowled at Seika and Buddy, but it was anyone's guess whether she was unhappy because she didn't have the day off like her sister, or something deeper.

When Carolyn asked about coffee and breakfast, Lotuse nodded her dark head and said, "Right away."

BY THE TIME CAROLYN and Adam finished breakfast and left for downtown, they saw that Lisa's car still wasn't in the garage.

"I wonder where she spent the night," Carolyn mused, "And who the lucky guy was."

"It might be worthwhile finding out," Adam answered. "Lisa might be a big help to someone able to glean information from her about the company. Innocent or not, she might be a vital link in this whole scenario.''

''You can't be serious. Lisa involved? She lives in her own little world of fashion, country clubs and high living. I'm betting there isn't a deceitful bone in her body.''

''Remind me never to take you to a racetrack,'' he responded wryly. ''Nothing is a sure bet. Not horses, and certainly not people.''

Carolyn fell silent. She liked Lisa. How could she function in her new role if everyone she met was suspect? For the first time in her life she had a chance to leave the past behind...but the scrapes and bruises on her body were a reminder that someone hated her enough to want her dead.

They used their security pass to enter a restricted area and were surprised to see a car in the spot labeled for Nick Calhoun. Adam decided they should check out the shipping department before tackling Della's office.

The burly Irishman was hunched at his desk. One eye was as black as soot, and his head shaved where a cut had been stitched. Carolyn involuntarily put a hand to her mouth when she saw him.

''You should have seen the other fellow,'' he quipped, and managed a lopsided grin with his fat lip.

''You shouldn't be here,'' Carolyn said, her professional training kicking in. ''You need time to heal. I'm surprised they let you out of the hospital.''

''I signed myself out. People die in hospitals. I'll take my chances on the outside.''

''Your chances don't look so good, Nick,'' Adam

answered frankly. "Want to tell us what happened?"

Nick muttered an oath. "Personal business. I'll handle it."

"Is that what you're doing here? Handling it?" Adam asked him bluntly.

"What kind of question is that?" Nick's eyes narrowed. "My getting beat up doesn't have anything to do with my job here." He shot Carolyn an anxious look. "You ain't about to fire me over this thing, are ya?"

"No, of course not, Nick," she said. "But surely someone else can keep on top of things for a few days while you recuperate."

"I'm telling ya, I'm fine and—" The rest of his words were cut off by the sharp ring of a fire alarm. "What in hell?"

He bounded from his chair, bolted out the door to a panel on the wall that showed all the locations of fire alarms. "It's in the package room!"

Adam grabbed a fire extinguisher in a glass case right outside Nick's door. "Call the fire department!"

"Security will do it. They have a monitor," Nick shouted over his shoulder.

At the door of the packaging department, Nick used his magnetized security card. A green light instantly responded. They flung open the door. Smoke in one corner of the huge room billowed to the ceiling.

Adam had the impression of a door closing at the other end of the long room, but a river of fire demanded his full attention as flames billowed high in one corner of the room. Nick grabbed another fire extinguisher, and between them they stopped the forward thrust of the fire.

Carolyn covered her mouth as she moved records, boxes and other papers away from where Adam and Nick were putting out the last embers of the fire. By the time they heard the shriek of a fire engine, it was all over.

The room had sustained very little damage. The fire had been confined to one area.

''What's your guess, Nick?'' Adam asked when they were back in his office. ''How do you think it started?''

''Hell, I don't know anything about all those pills and liquids they put in them boxes. I keep my nose out of that packaging department. I couldn't even tell you who all works there.''

The way he broke eye contact and pretended total ignorance sent Adam's intuitive antennae quivering.

The man was lying.

Chapter Twelve

The impression Adam had of a hurried movement at the far end of the room kept nagging at him. He really hadn't seen anything that could be identified as someone fleeing the scene, and the smoke could have blurred his vision.

As the firemen were cleaning up, Adam asked the chief if he thought the fire had been deliberately set.

"Can't say for sure without more checking," the burly man responded. "But if you want my off-the-cuff opinion, it does looks like arson. The way the fire erupted in one corner where some boxes were piled is suspect. The whole thing looks hurried and inept. There's little chance that the whole building would have been burned down from that localized area."

Carolyn remained quiet during the exchange and let Adam handle all the interaction with the firemen. She certainly didn't want attention focused on her as the primary stockholder in the company.

He was concerned about the same thing. If the newspapers got a whiff of possible arson, the media attention on Horizon could hamper his investigation. As soon as he could, he had to find out exactly what was in those boxes. A pile of ashes didn't promise much enlightenment.

Nick stomped around, blustering and swearing. He swore that it must have been some internal combustion in one of the boxes that caused it and was furious that his shipping department had been threatened.

"The whole building could have gone up in flames. No fool would set something like that. If I hadn't come in this morning, the whole place could have burned down," he fumed, dismissing Adam's part in putting out the fire.

Adam and Carolyn talked to the security guard who'd made rounds an hour earlier. He assured them he'd seen nothing suspicious when he punched his clock in the packaging room an hour earlier.

"Who's going to call the Dragon Lady, I mean, Mrs. Denison, and tell her what happened?" the guard asked, obviously hoping it wasn't going to be him.

With just about as much enthusiasm, Carolyn answered, "I'll do it."

They went into her office to make the call, and since they didn't have the telephone number of the mountain home, Carolyn had to call the mansion for it.

Morna acted as if she'd been appointed guardian of the couple's privacy. "They're not to be disturbed by any business calls. I have my orders."

"Well, I'm giving you another order, Morna. From now on, when I ask for information of any kind, you will give it to me, is that understood? And I'll do the deciding whether they should be disturbed or not.'' There was a pause. Then she wrote down the number and hung up.

Adam was surprised. This was the first time he'd glimpsed Carolyn's firm command of people. Her grandfather had chosen well, he decided. Once Carolyn got her feet squarely planted on the ground, she'd take over from Della and prove her worth. *And move out of your reach forever,* a mocking inner voice reminded him. He shoved the truth away, but a sudden sense of loss had already made itself known.

''Wow, the pretty lady has an iron fist,'' Adam said. ''I'm betting you won't have any more trouble with Morna's knowing who's boss.''

''A hospital is a good training ground. You can't let yourself be manipulated by the staff in matters that aren't negotiable.'' She took a deep breath, ''Well, here goes.''

No one answered the phone on the first five rings, and Carolyn was about to hang up when Della issued a curt ''Hello.'' It was clear she was annoyed by the call.

''It's Carolyn.''

''Carolyn?'' she repeated, surprised or annoyed, Carolyn couldn't tell which.

''Sorry for the interruption, Della. I'm calling because there's a matter I felt you should know about right away. This morning there was a small fire at the company headquarters.''

''A fire?'' she echoed as if not sure she'd understood correctly.

''Nothing major, Della,'' Carolyn quickly told her. ''Some boxes were destroyed in the packaging department, and there's some fire damage in one corner of the room. The firemen haven't determined how it started.''

''And they called you?'' Her tone was laced with resentment.

''Nick, Adam and I were on the scene.''

''What were you doing at the company on Sunday morning?'' Della demanded, as if Carolyn's presence there was somehow responsible for what had happened.

''I thought I'd get settled in my office,'' Carolyn lied. ''There's no need for you and Jasper to rush back. Everything is under control. I'll call you if anything further develops.''

''We'll be back this afternoon,'' Della said flatly, and hung up without even saying goodbye.

''That was fun,'' Carolyn said sarcastically. ''I don't know how I'm going to ease myself into management when Della and Jasper are determined to keep treating me like an unwelcome outsider.''

''Simple. You hold the purse strings.'' He came up behind her and drew her back against him as they looked out the window. In the distance they could see Mount Rainier, nearly a hundred miles away, and the glimmering waters of Lake Washington filled with Sunday sailors.

''There's no way I can become CEO of this company unless I learn how it operates from the ground up.''

''Your grandfather left you controlling interest in Horizon for a good reason, Carolyn. He knew you were a fighter.''

I can't do this alone. Unable to deny a rising need, she turned around. *I need you with me.* Ignoring the protesting ache in her arm muscles, she put them around his neck. Her lips parted as they boldly claimed his. The kiss was like a firebrand.

Adam responded the way a starving man welcomed nourishment. His hands traced the curves of her back, and he drew her against the hard length of his body. As her fingers threaded through his thick hair, their kisses sought fulfillment of the desire humming through them. Adam knew that if he didn't stop kissing and caressing her, the fragile boundary they'd agreed on would be crossed. He sensed she had had this burst of passion out of a need that wasn't wholly a commitment to him or the pretense they'd been struggling to maintain. She was frightened. She needed reassurance.

Slowly withdrawing from their embrace, he tried to disguise the truth that he wanted her so badly he was using every ounce of willpower to set her away from him. If things had been different, he would have locked the office door and given in completely to passion. But he knew that the happenings of last night and this morning had made her vulnerable.

He opened his mouth to speak, but she put a finger over his lips. "Don't. Don't say anything. Let it be."

She turned away from the window and walked back to her desk. She didn't want what they'd shared to be ruined by words. Taking a deep breath, she asked, "Now what?"

"Let's get in the car and do a little checking."

"Checking what?"

"I've been keeping a log of names and addresses of possible suspects inside the company. Let's find out who's home on this Sunday morning and who isn't."

Already Adam had started considering who might have let themselves into the building and set the fire.

"Sounds like a good idea," agreed Carolyn, grateful to have something constructive to do. She didn't know what had come over her. She couldn't believe she'd initiated the passionate moment that had nearly ended with them on the couch. "You drive. Who's first on the list?"

"Cliff."

She wasn't surprised. As long as she'd known Cliff, he'd always been an opportunist. She suspected that if it suited his purposes, he'd be willing to burn down the whole place and laugh off the consequences.

"But why would he do it?" she mused. "Do you think I backed him into some kind of a corner by threatening to drag his past into view?"

Adam didn't have an answer.

Cliff's address was a whitewashed apartment building set close to the street, with only a narrow strip of grass bordering the front. The parking lot at the side was full, so Adam parked across the street in view of all the front windows.

"What excuse are we going to give for showing up on his doorstep?" Carolyn asked anxiously, fighting a sudden onset of cowardice. "Maybe you should go and I'll stay in the car."

"That might be best," he agreed. "You've had a plateful of excitement already today." When he took her hand, he realized it was damp with perspiration. Almost run over last night and arson this morning. She wasn't used to this.

Furious that someone was putting her through this hell, he promised, "Whoever's behind this is going to make a mistake, Carolyn. When he does, I'll personally exact payment for every anxious moment he's caused you.''

Her expression relaxed. ''And I'll be second in line to collect.''

''Good girl. Now let's see if I can find out if Cliff is spending a quiet Sunday morning at home. If he is there and invites me in, I may stay a little while to chat.''

''I thought we were just going to check and see if he was home?'' she protested. Maybe staying in the car wasn't such a hot idea.

When Adam didn't answer, she followed his gaze and saw what had caught his attention. Someone was coming out of the apartment building. As the front door swung open and they saw who it was, Carolyn gasped.

But there was no mistaking the petite, dark-haired woman who was smiling up at Cliff in her coquettish way.

Lisa!

''I don't believe it,'' Carolyn said in dismay.

''Well, I guess we know why she didn't come home last night,'' Adam responded dryly.

They watched as Cliff walked Lisa to her car, which was parked at the side of the building. He gave her a brief kiss and then waved as she backed out of the lot.

They watched as Cliff took out his cell phone the moment Lisa was out of sight and stood there talking to someone for a couple of minutes. After he'd finished his conversation, he casually stuck his hands in his pockets and strolled down the sidewalk as if about to enjoy a walk on this clear Sunday morning.

"Well, I guess we got the answer to our question. It wasn't Cliff who set the fire," Adam said. "He was too busy lighting a different kind of his own."

"The whole thing makes me sick to my stomach. Lisa. Can't she see him for what he is? Pure scum!"

"Come on, let's tail Cliff for a while and see where he goes. Maybe he's meeting someone. We know he didn't set the fire, but he might have arranged for someone else to do it."

They left her car parked where it was and joined a few other pedestrians on the sidewalk, keeping a concealing distance behind Cliff as he sauntered down the street. Carolyn shivered, and not from the briskness of the early-morning air.

"Why would Lisa take up with someone like Cliff? It doesn't make sense. They don't run in the same circles, and the only thing they have in common is their connection to Horizon."

"Exactly," Adam said.

She shot him a look. "You think that the two of them are involved in what's going on with the illicit shipments at Horizon?"

"It's a possibility. Cliff could be using Lisa to gain the information he needs. She might be completely innocent or part of the operation. One thing I do know—both of them love money, and neither has any visible means of acquiring it."

"I would believe anything of Cliff, but not Lisa," Carolyn declared as if swayed by her loyalty to the one friend she'd made in this situation. "It makes me sick to think she's taken up with him. If she only knew…"

"You're not going to tell her a thing," Adam warned. "We'll let this thing play out, see where it takes us. I wish I could handle all this without your help, Carolyn, but I can't," he said regretfully. "This whole investigation would fall apart without you at the center of it."

She managed a weak smile. "It's nice to feel indispensable, but I could settle for something a little less demanding, thank you." She hooked her arm through his. "The truth is, I'm finding out some interesting things about myself. And about you."

"Really? And how do I measure up?"

"I think you know the answer to that." She felt heat rising in her cheeks.

He saw the blush and knew that she was referring to her initiation of the intimacy back at the office. He was about to tell her how much just being with her had added to his life, but caught himself. This was not the time or place. Sadly he wasn't sure that there would ever be a time or place.

They followed Cliff to a bakery, a grocery store and a liquor store. Armed with his purchases, he returned to his apartment without having had any personal contact with anyone. Was he doing his weekly shopping or getting ready for company?

"Now what?" Carolyn asked, hoping that Adam wouldn't decide they should pay Cliff a visit. She didn't know if she could keep Lisa out of the conversation. It still rankled her that Cliff had pulled the woman into his sordid life.

"Let's get back in the car." If Adam had been alone, he probably would have staked out the apartment himself. Instead, he made a call to a junior agent and gave him the duty. If someone showed up in answer to Cliff's call, Adam wanted to know about it.

Carolyn searched Adam's face as he started the car and headed south. "Who's next?"

"Nellie Ryan. If something fishy is going on in the packaging and shipping departments, I don't see how she could miss it."

"Maybe she's turning a blind eye to it because of her feelings for Nick," Carolyn offered.

Adam gave her an approving smile. "Bingo."

Nellie was home all right, and from the looks of her gardening clothes as she knelt in a front garden, trowel in hand and empty flowerpots surrounding her, she'd been hard at it all morning.

Right off, she told them that she'd had a call from Nick about the fire and started asking them more questions. When she suggested coffee on her red-wood deck while they talked, they readily accepted her invitation. Her home was a two-storied, modest place and surrounded with trees, shrubs and flowers.

"Nick said they think the fire was set," she confided as she poured three mugs of coffee and offered them slices of lemon cake.

"Maybe it was a disgruntled employee," Adam suggested, using a red herring. "Can you think of anyone in the packaging department bent on revenge?"

"Heavens, no. I would have heard any scuttlebutt about someone angry enough to try and burn the place down. I know that Elinor runs a tight ship, but this kind of thing in her department is beyond belief."

"Maybe she fouled up on some of the orders and needed to hide her guilt," Carolyn suggested.

"Not Elinor," Nellie scoffed. "She could hide any mistake in her department in a dozen different ways without anyone being the wiser. She sure as heck wouldn't set fire to the place, and I wouldn't want to be around when she gets the news. That department is her life."

"And Elinor's never said a word about any confrontations in her department?" Adam asked.

"No, Elinor is good with people, and she's a hard worker. I hope she isn't going to get into trouble over this."

"You're in and out of the packaging department all the time, aren't you? After the orders are boxed for shipping, is there any special arrangement for handling them?"

"I don't know. You'll have to ask Elinor," she said flatly. "I have enough of a challenge keeping the production department running smoothly."

"We were surprised to find Nick at work this morning," Carolyn said, changing the subject. "I really think he's pushing it, Nellie. Can't you get him to take care of himself?"

She sighed. "I wish I could, but..." She chewed her lower lip. "Nick's got himself in a peck of trouble. I suppose I shouldn't say anything, but it's his gambling. Every week he goes to these poker games and gets himself in deeper and deeper."

"You think somebody's getting violent about collecting?" Adam asked.

"Who else would beat him up like that? Everyone likes Nick." She blushed as she added, "Some of us more than others."

"He seems like a nice man," Carolyn offered.

They chatted a few more minutes with her, refused more coffee and took their leave.

"Well, I guess we can cross her name off," Carolyn said as they drove back to the center of town.

"Maybe not."

Carolyn looked at him with raised eyebrows. "You have to be kidding."

"While we were checking Cliff out, Nellie would have had plenty of time to get back home and throw on some gardening clothes. Maybe Nick told her about the fire, but there's the possibility that she already knew."

"You're suspicious of everyone, aren't you?" Carolyn said, a stirring of regret in her voice. She knew what it was like to keep your guard up all the time. "You don't trust anyone, do you."

He shot her a quick smile. "Present company excepted. What about you?"

She knew he was inviting the same kind of reassurance, but her uncertainty about "Angel" lingered. During those years she'd been shuttled from one foster home to another, she'd learned not to put a lot of faith in what people told you. Could she honestly say she trusted Adam with all her heart and soul? Her answer must have been written on her face.

"That's what I thought," he said, and gave his attention to his driving.

She'd assumed they were returning to Horizon, and when he turned in a different direction, she asked, "Where are we going now?"

"Susan Kimble's place," he said. "Maybe she's the one Cliff is expecting to share his food and liquor."

"Don't you buy the 'just friends' tag?"

"Do you?" Adam asked. "You know the guy better than I do."

She searched her memory for any platonic relationships Cliff had had while in medical school. "There was one rather plain girl in the chemistry class he was nice to. At the time I suspected she was sharing her homework with him."

Adam just grunted as if she'd proved his point. He turned onto a backstreet and stopped in front of a small house on a narrow lot.

"Well, I guess Susan's home," Carolyn said. "Her car's in the driveway."

"Let's find out."

They knocked on the door several times, but there was no answer. They could hear a small dog yapping from somewhere outside the house, and as they turned to leave, they saw it in the backyard.

It was a puppy, and it was jumping at the gate with such force that suddenly one of the rickety posts gave way, tipping enough to one side to allow the dog to squeeze through. It bounded down the driveway like a freed prisoner, leaping and barking all around them.

"Whoa, fellow, whoa." Adam laughingly tried to defend himself from the dog's exuberant greeting. Adam picked up the pup and held it firmly as he received an enthusiastic face wash from the pup's tongue. "Sorry, little guy, but you've got to go back in the yard."

Carolyn chuckled. She could tell that Adam was taken with the dog, and she wondered if he'd ever had a dog of his own. From what he'd said about his upper-class background, she guessed a smelly puppy probably wasn't in the picture.

Adam studied the splintered post. "You hold the gate shut," he told Carolyn as he set the dog down. "I'll look around for something to brace it shut."

There was some laundry hanging on a clothesline and some wooden stakes lying near a small vegetable garden. He'd just started across the lawn to check them out when he smelled it.

"What the...?" He walked quickly to the back door.

Gas! The smell of it seeping through the cracks around the door was unmistakable. He bolted to a kitchen window and peered in. The thin figure of Susan Kimble was lying on the floor in front of a gas stove.

"Stay back," he yelled at Carolyn, who was still standing by the gate to keep the puppy from escaping again.

"What is it?" she asked as she saw him grab a rake that was leaning against the house and begin breaking windows in the kitchen and laundry room. As the gas-filled air poured out, she had her answer.

Adam jerked a towel off the clothesline, held it over his nose and mouth and ran to the back door.

It wasn't locked.

As the strong odor of gas assaulted him, he rushed into the kitchen.

Susan Kimble was positioned directly in front of the stove, and the gas jets had been turned on full blast. He twisted them off, then picked her up and carried her out into the yard, his chest heaving with a spasm of coughing.

Carolyn knelt beside the young woman. She sought a spark of life, even though she'd known the truth from the instant she'd seen her.

They were too late. Susan Kimble was dead.

Chapter Thirteen

When the paramedics arrived, they told Carolyn and Adam what they already knew. Susan Kimble had been asphyxiated. Was it by her own hand or someone else's? Adam immediately wondered.

They had their answer when a note fastened with a hummingbird magnet on the door of the refrigerator was discovered. It was handwritten.

"I'm doing this because it's too late to make things right. The guilt is mine. My weakness. Forgive me. Susan."

The arrival of the ambulance had caused a neighbor, Mrs. Reilly, to rush over to see what the commotion was about. Carolyn was relieved to learn that she was the one who'd given Susan the puppy and was willing to take it back.

When the coroner and two policemen arrived, Carolyn and Adam explained how they had dropped by Susan's house for a visit and found the body in the gas-filled house. Carolyn identified herself as Susan's employer, and Adam as her husband. They didn't say anything about their real reason for the visit and didn't mention the fire.

"It's better not to feed any idle speculation,"

Adam said when they were in the car and driving away. "Maybe Susan set the fire and maybe she didn't. Obviously, from her note, she's remorseful about something."

"Maybe it was about her being pregnant," Carolyn said evenly.

Adam shot Carolyn a wide-eyed look. "Are you serious?"

"About three months, I'd say. Her extended uterus was apparent when I was checking for vital signs. I'm sure the coroner will confirm it. And they can determine the father through tests." Carolyn's mouth tightened. "But I doubt if anyone will push the issue of paternity."

Adam knew he couldn't request such tests. He didn't have any evidence that linked Susan's personal life to his investigation. There wasn't anything connecting her to the fire or to any participation in the illegal shipment of drugs. It was certainly true that Susan had been in the right place in the business department to expedite false orders after someone initiated them, but who that person was remained a mystery. And how did those orders get through all the checks and balances of each department?

"Do you want to go back to Horizon?" Adam asked Carolyn as she sat rigid in the seat beside him. "Or would you like to stop for lunch?"

She shook her head. "I'm not hungry. I need a little time to assimilate all that's happened, I guess. Why don't you drop me off at the house? I'll be a lady of leisure this afternoon, and you'll be free to spend the time however you want."

"Promise me you'll stay put in the house? I don't

want you wandering around anywhere without me. The jealous husband, you know.'' He winked at her.

She appreciated his effort to make light of the situation. ''It's a deal. I'll be the dutiful little wife and keep the home fires burning.''

It was a poor choice of words, she realized. All the unanswered questions about the morning's ordeal came flooding back.

''Maybe you should just keep the bed warm for me,'' he suggested quickly, deliberately trying to shift her thoughts in a different direction.

''Is that a dare?'' she challenged.

''More of a hope,'' he said honestly, and was rewarded by a slight flush on her pale cheeks. The thought of her waiting in that huge bed, her arms open wide to receive him, sent a rush of desire through him. He cursed the sadistic fates that were causing him to fall in love with a woman he couldn't have. His life of danger and uncertainty had already jeopardized her well-being, he'd be a fool to think she'd want anything to do with him after this was over.

When they reached the mansion and made their way to their wing, he was tempted to stay there with her, but an urgency to pursue the new developments of the fire and Susan's suicide won out.

''I wouldn't be surprised if Della and Jasper go straight to Horizon when they get into town,'' he told Carolyn as he freshened up and made preparations to leave. ''You can call me there if you need me. Lisa's car is gone and Buddy is out on his boat, so nobody else is home. You can do as you please. I'll be back before dinner.''

''Be careful,'' she said, trying to keep her voice

steady as she sat on the edge of the bed watching him. Never had the trite phrase seemed so weighted. Her chest tightened with the nagging fear that some nebulous danger would overtake him the minute he was out of her sight. Everything about him dominated her senses. She longed to touch the wave of dark hair falling over his forehead and trace the strong lines of his chin. The tempting curves of his mouth brought back memories that made her voice husky as she said, "Maybe I should go with you."

He eased down beside her and turned her face gently toward his. "Hey, don't look so worried. What happened today, even our narrow escape last night, can be very helpful to us, because it means that the situation is no longer stagnant. As long as there is movement, unexpected facts will surface, and there'll be opportunities to discover things that someone wants to keep hidden. That's the name of the game."

"I don't want to play," she said flatly.

He laughed, and his gaze was suddenly like a warm caress on her face. "You're precious. Remind me to ask you to marry me."

"Remind me to say yes."

Was she was just following his banter or inviting him to take her seriously? He couldn't be sure. In any case, this wasn't the time to pursue it, he told himself. Before this investigation was over, she could very well hate the sight of him. He pressed a whisper of a kiss to her forehead.

"Try to enjoy the rest of the day," he said. "You might even make use of the swimming pool and Jacuzzi to ease those sore muscles."

"And show off all my scrapes and bruises? I

don't think so. But don't worry, I'll make use of the free afternoon.''

In his work, Adam had learned to look beyond the surface of words. A slight inflection could reveal more than what a person was saying. Carolyn had already decided on what she was going to do. He was sure of it.

''What do you have in mind?'' he asked casually as he stood up and looked down at her. She showed a flicker of hesitation before she answered.

''I'm going to check out the attic. Morna said they stored my grandfather's things there when they made his rooms ready for us. No, I don't need your help,'' she added before he had a chance to say anything. ''I'm just looking for personal things. Maybe something about my mother. Those snapshots of Jasper's weren't very satisfying.''

''I'm not sure you should go through that stuff alone.''

''Why not?''

He could tell from the jut of her chin that any argument was useless. Carolyn had made up her mind to spend the afternoon in the attic and that was that. He could understand why she didn't want her emotions on parade. If there was any crying to be done, she'd rather do it alone. Still, he wished he'd handled the situation differently.

''Well, don't overdo it,'' he cautioned.

''I won't,'' she promised. ''And if I find anything that looks like business stuff, I'll set it aside and we'll take a closer look at it later.''

Her tone was dismissive. There was nothing he could do but turn, leave the room and hope with all his heart that her search would bring the emotional healing she deserved.

CAROLYN FOUND MORNA in the dining room giving Lotuse instructions about setting the table for the evening meal. The housekeeper's expression was anything but welcoming, and she visibly stiffened as if the enemy had arrived.

Morna reminded Carolyn of one of the unfriendly floor supervisors at the hospital who treated everyone on her ward—doctors, nurses and visitors alike—with cold disdain. Carolyn had learned to ignore the woman's hostility. She drew on the experience now as she faced the glowering housekeeper.

"Morna, I've decided to spend some time in the attic this afternoon," Carolyn told her without preamble. "I'll need someone to show me where my grandfather's personal belongings are stored."

"It's Sunday afternoon," Morna replied as if Carolyn was not aware of that fact. "Another day for that kind of activity might serve everyone better."

"It might," Carolyn agreed evenly. "But I've decided to do it this afternoon."

As if controlling an overwhelming urge to flatly refuse Carolyn's request, Morna clamped her mouth shut. Her silent, steely stare didn't waver for a long moment, but finally she said in clipped tones, "I'll call Mack in from the greenhouse. I guess his work there will just have to be put off."

Carolyn ignored the pointed censure in her tone. "I'll wait in the morning room."

It was obvious from Mack's appearance and poignant scent that he'd been working with dirt and fertilizer. He wiped his hands on his soiled overalls.

"Morna said you were wanting me. Is there something wrong? She was in a real huff. I know I'm a little behind in getting those shrubs trimmed and—"

Carolyn said quickly, "Everything's fine, Mack. You're doing a wonderful job with the landscaping. I just need your help for a few minutes."

She explained her plans to spend the afternoon in the attic and asked him to help her locate some of her grandfather's personal effects.

Relief spread across Mack's smudged face, and he led the way to an attic staircase located in the middle of the second floor. After searching for the right key on a ring hanging from his belt, he opened the squeaky door, reached in and turned on a light. Then he stepped back to let her enter first.

A low, peaked-ceiling room stretched away in every direction. The front and back walls of the attic had a series of dormer windows.

She gasped at the stacks of boxes, barrels, trunks, assorted furniture and other household items haphazardly spread before her. She'd never seen anything like it. It would take days, no, weeks, to sort out all the stuff.

"Kind of a mess," Mack granted. "I guess the family's been shoving stuff up here for a good many years. That's the way it is with these old houses, you know."

Carolyn didn't know. She'd never had a family. And she'd never had a house. She felt like an intruder. What right did she have to be there, looking through other people's belongings?

"I think we piled all your grandfather's things over by that first window. Arthur didn't have a lot of clothes. Mostly books, papers and things from his bedroom and study," Mack said as he forged a path through the maze of items. "Why don't you point out what you want and I'll move them downstairs?"

"I have no idea what I want," she answered honestly. "If I decide to move anything, Mack, I'll let you know. There's enough light from the windows for me to check out some of the boxes." She gestured at an old footstool. "I'll just sit here and go through them."

"Okay, let me open these boxes for you. That way you won't have any trouble looking to see what's in them."

"Thank you, Mack. Looks as if I'll be busy most of the afternoon."

"All right, then. I'll be getting back to my work." He hesitated. "Are you sure you don't want me to send up one of the girls to help?"

She shook her head. "No, I think this is something I have to do by myself."

After he'd gone, Carolyn wondered why she'd been so stubborn about doing this all alone. She'd never been one to believe in lingering spirits, but in that shadowy attic, she felt the back of her neck prickle.

Her fingers trembled slightly as she examined some of the things that had been her grandfather's. She stroked a pipe that still retained a strong odor of tobacco and turned the pages of old books that had his name in them. Little by little she began to know intimate things about him: he loved reading, smoked a pipe, and collected small, wooden Indian figures.

She went through several other boxes Mack had opened for her, but found only miscellaneous things, like papers and magazines her grandfather had kept for some reason. Nothing personal. Nothing that would ease her sense of disconnection. She'd about given up when she opened a box of framed photographs. Her mouth went dry and her hands trembled as she drew them out one by one.

There was a photograph of Arthur and his wife in their wedding finery. *My grandmother.* Carolyn stared at their faces for a long time and then put the frame down with a sigh. They were two strangers staring at her, nothing more.

There was a high school graduation photo of Jasper, showing him as a solemn young man. Carolyn wondered why he looked as if life had always been a heavy burden. In a silver frame at the bottom of the box was the photograph she'd been hoping for. Her hands trembled as she picked up a picture of a smiling, honey-blond adolescent girl.

As Carolyn read the inscription, "To Daddy, with love, Alicia," all the years of displacement rushed over her with an aching loneliness. She blinked rapidly to clear her eyes of an instant fullness. When she was a child, the words *mother* and *father* had always reminded her of the void in her life. Now with a trembling finger, she traced the features that were so like hers. She sought to find comfort in this realization of her identity, but to no avail.

"Mother," she whispered in a husky voice, but it was only a word. There were no memories to give it meaning. "It's too late," she said in a tremulous voice. "It's too late."

She suddenly became aware of the sound of footfalls. Quickly she put the picture down, stood up and swiped at her tear-filled eyes.

"Adam?" she asked in disbelief when he came into view. Was she hallucinating?

"There you are," he said. "I thought I heard sounds coming from this corner."

"What…what are you doing here?"

"I'm really not sure," he admitted, but as light from the window bathed her tear-streaked face, he knew his intuition had been right. Giving in to a nagging feeling that nothing was more important at that moment than being with her, he had turned the car around before he reached Horizon. "I guess I decided you might need a hug."

He put his arms around her, but she stiffened, fearful that if he touched her, she'd give way to the shattering emotion within her. She pulled away and sat back down on her footstool.

"It's been a little draining going through this stuff," she admitted as she picked up the photograph of Alicia and handed it to him. "This must have been taken about the time she ran away with my father."

He nodded. "Yes, I'd say she was about sixteen, wouldn't you?"

Carolyn's controlled voice and manner didn't fool him one bit. He could tell she was torn up inside and fighting for composure. As he looked at the picture of Alicia, he could see the physical resemblance between mother and daughter. Even though strength radiated from the clear, direct gazes of both, Adam was certain of one difference between them: Carolyn would control her future, not waste it.

"I'm almost to the bottom of this box," she said as she took out the last remaining large envelope filled with various sizes of snapshots. As they spilled out onto her lap, her stomach took a sickening plunge. No, it couldn't be! All of them were of her—as an adult!

As she played them through her fingers, the photos were a kaleidoscope of her life. Someone had documented every area of her life for the past five years. There were pictures of her walking the hospital corridors, checking medical charts, coming out of the Friends Free Clinic, climbing the outdoor stairs to her apartment, shopping with Rosie, working at her desk at the investment company and many, many more taken in almost every area of her life.

She was stunned, horrified and angry at this unbelievable evidence of the invasion of her privacy. Her grandfather was the one responsible. He'd hired someone to spy on her and knew everything about her. Instead of openly admitting to their relationship, he'd been too cowardly to show himself.

She gave the photos an angry shove, spilling them all over the floor.

"Easy, easy," Adam soothed, hiding his own astonishment that Arthur must have paid someone a bundle to keep a surveillance on Carolyn for all those years.

"My grandfather can take his blasted house and pharmaceutical firm, and... He withheld from me the only thing that mattered. He was afraid to love me for myself." Tears spilled down her cheeks. "He had to make sure I was worthy to be a Stanford. Well, I'm not! And nothing I've seen or heard makes me want to be."

She jerked away from Adam's hand on her arm, pushed her way through the attic clutter and bounded down the attic stairs. She was consumed by an irrational urge to get as far away as she could from the pain in her heart. In her confused state, she turned the wrong way on the second floor and realized too late that she was headed for Della and Jasper's wing.

She stopped short, swung around and bumped into Adam. Frustration brought hot tears to her eyes. She hadn't realized he'd been behind her as she fled. Without saying anything, he put his arms around her, and her wild urge to run away faded. Adam led the way back to their rooms and firmly closed the door behind them.

As he looked at her with tender, loving concern, she realized with a start that he wasn't judging her irrational behavior at all. She didn't have to role-play with him, hide her true feelings, or apologize for her emotional display. It was an experience she'd never had before with anyone. Her defense mechanism had always fallen into place when she was about to reveal her inner thoughts to someone.

A muscle flicked in his cheek as he moved closer to her. "It was Arthur's loss that he lacked the courage to claim you and love you," he said gently. "I think your grandfather knew that when he made his new will. If he'd lived, I believe he would have eventually drawn you into his life and been rewarded by knowing what a treasure you are."

"Thank you," she said, her eyes moist.

"Would you like that hug now?" he asked.

She nodded. His arms went around her, holding her gently and firmly until she raised her lips to his. He searched her face before he tightened his embrace and gave her a long, exploring kiss that left them both breathless. Then he buried his lips against the quickening pulse in her neck. Carolyn gasped as the flick of his tongue on her skin fanned the fire between them. She returned his kisses with an urgency that drove all thought from her mind.

When he lifted his mouth from hers, his eyes asked if she wanted him to stop. Her answer was to lace her arms around his neck and to offer him her lips again.

She clung to him when he lifted her up and carried her to the bed. Their clothes fell away and she welcomed the hands that moved caressingly over her, heightening the pleasure of his kisses. Trembling in his arms, tracing the length of his inviting body with her hands, she matched his rising hunger.

Never had she imagined the incredible sensations she felt as they made love—giving, taking and sharing. For the first time in her life, Carolyn realized the fulfillment of an unconditional love.

And when their desire had been lovingly sated, Carolyn sighed with contentment and nestled more deeply in his loving arms.

"What was that sigh all about?" he asked as he nuzzled her cheek.

"I was just thinking that my wedding night was slow in coming," she answered as she turned to him again. "But it was well worth the wait."

Chapter Fourteen

They were late coming down for dinner. Lisa was the only one sitting at the dining-room table, which was set for six, and she gave them a knowing smile as if signs of their shared passion lingered on their faces.

"Some things are better than eating, right?" she teased, winking at Carolyn.

"Right," Adam agreed, and turned to Carolyn with a smile that spoke volumes. Her eyes were soft and loving as he held out a chair for her. *Carolyn. Sweet Carolyn.* The past two hours had taken him into a different realm of feeling and being, fired senses with a passion he'd never known before. Although his marriage had been good, he'd never enjoyed the height of total bliss in bed that he experienced with Carolyn. He was no longer a pretend husband. He vowed that he would commit himself on every level to her happiness if she made the decision to keep him in her life.

As Lotuse began to serve dinner, Adam smiled at Lisa. "And how did you spend your Sunday?" he asked as if he had no idea where she'd been this morning and probably last night.

"Visiting a friend," she answered without the least hesitation. "And this afternoon I played a round of golf at the club. What about you two? Don't tell me you spent a beautiful day like this at Horizon."

"Only part of the day," Carolyn answered. "Didn't Morna tell you that there was a small fire there this morning?"

"What?" Lisa set her wineglass down with a splash. "Where? How?"

Either she was a consummate actress or she really didn't know about the fire, Adam decided as he briefly explained what had happened.

"I can't believe it. Do Mom and Jasper know?"

"I called them," Carolyn said. "That's probably why they're late."

"I bet she's going to be in a snit," Lisa said with a groan. "She protects that place like a mother bear. I'd hate to be in the shoes of the nut who set it."

"Do you have any idea who it might have been?" Carolyn asked in what she hoped was a casual tone. "I mean, has your mother said anything about a disgruntled employee or competitor, someone who might be seeking revenge?"

"She never tells me anything about the business," Lisa replied. "I've offered plenty of times to try my hand at working there, but she doesn't want me around." The bitter note in her voice was hard to miss, but she tried to cover it with a laugh. "So I guess I'll just go on being her pampered daughter."

Adam tried a few more innocent questions without gleaning any helpful information.

A few minutes later, just as Lotuse was removing

the soup bowls, Della and Jasper walked into the dining room. Lisa immediately began to plague her mother with questions about the fire, but it was obvious Della didn't want to talk about it.

"Everything is under control," she said in a tone that didn't invite further discussion on the subject.

"The dinner table is not the place for discussing problems and indulging in unpleasant conversation," Jasper stated in his usual unsociable manner, and his glare included Carolyn and Adam in the pronouncement.

Carolyn was surprised at their attitude. She'd have thought they'd be asking Adam and her about the fire, since they were on the scene. Did Della and Jasper know about Susan Kimble's suicide? Should she say something or let it ride?

Adam's thoughts were running along the same channel. Would Susan's death mean anything more to Della than the loss of a business manager? It was becoming apparent that several people at Horizon had to be involved in the illegal packaging and shipment of drugs to black markets. If Susan had been one of those people in the chain, and if Della was orchestrating these undercover sales, she would have lost an important accomplice. What would she do now? Close up the operation? Or find a replacement?

A heavy silence settled over the dinner table, and Carolyn was sorry Buddy wasn't there to liven things up. Lisa seemed sullen, and Carolyn wondered if the mood had anything to do with Cliff. It was all she could do to pretend ignorance when she wanted more than anything to warn Lisa not to get involved with the creep.

The expected telephone call about Susan's suicide came just as they were finishing dessert, and Della lashed out at Morna for the interruption. "Tell them I'll call back," she ordered.

"It sounds important," Morna insisted. "Something about a news release."

"Dammit," Jasper said. "Somebody's been blabbing about the fire." The pointed look he gave Carolyn and Adam made it clear who he thought was responsible.

Della lips tightened. "Morna, bring me the phone. I guess we all may as well hear what some reporter's take is on the fire. No doubt the facts have been embellished to create a more exciting story." Morna handed her the phone, and Della answered with a curt, "Yes."

Adam watched the frown on her face change to one of utter dismay. Her eyes widened, and her breathing quickened as she listened. The caller must have mentioned Carolyn and Adam's name, because her horrified gaze swung in their direction.

Her voice was strained. "Yes, thank you for calling. I didn't know," she said, and hung up.

"What is it, Mother? Is it Buddy? Something's happened to Buddy, hasn't it?" Lisa demanded fearfully.

"No, it's not Buddy."

"Then what?"

Della leveled her malevolent gaze at Carolyn and Adam. "Why don't one of you tell her? Apparently you two had front-row seats."

"Who was on the phone, Della?" Jasper demanded as the lines in his angular face deepened. "What's this all about?"

Adam answered evenly, "I assume that the call was about Susan Kimble."

"What about her?" Jasper demanded. "Don't tell me she's involved in setting the fire!"

"This isn't about the fire," Della snapped. "Susan committed suicide this afternoon. Carolyn and Adam found her. And they didn't say a word about it." Della's eyes were fiery pinpoints. "I find it incomprehensible that they waited for someone else to tell us."

"Is this true?" Jasper demanded. "Carolyn, may I ask why you sat here all through dinner without informing us?"

"We were honoring your dictates, Uncle Jasper," Carolyn said, meeting his eyes unwaveringly. "If I remember rightly, you informed us that the dinner table was no place for indulging in unpleasant conversation. I find the suicide of a nice young woman very unpleasant, don't you?"

He shoved back his dessert plate. "Your lack of judgment, Carolyn, dismays me."

Eyes flashing, Lisa turned on Jasper as if she'd been waiting for such an opportunity to say her piece. "What gives you the right to decide what we can or cannot say at the dinner table? You've never been the one paying the bills. Arthur kept you just the way he kept the rest of us. And now it's Carolyn who's keeping us. This is her house, her food and her table. If she kicks all of us out, you'll be the one to blame."

"Lisa!" her mother cried. "Apologize."

"No," Lisa said, and shoved back her chair. "And I may as well tell you now—I have plans for moving out. I've found someone, and I don't give a damn whether any of you approve of him or not."

Carolyn's stomach turned over. *Cliff. No, Lisa, no,* Carolyn pleaded silently. *Don't settle for someone who will exploit you, break your heart and dump you before you even know what happened.*

Lisa stomped out of the room, and Carolyn expected her mother to follow, but she didn't. Della acted as if her daughter's pronouncement was nothing but a temper tantrum. She was more interested in grilling Carolyn and Adam.

"What were you doing at Susan's house?" Della demanded. "And Nellie's? She's the one who called. Why are you two going behind my back? Contacting *my* loyal employees at their homes?"

Adam surprised Carolyn by telling Della the truth. "We thought they might know who set the fire."

"Isn't that the job of the police? I see no cause for you to be interfering with their investigation. And look what happened!" she said angrily. "Now media attention is centered on Horizon because of you."

"And that's a bad thing?" Adam asked. "Why?"

She swallowed. "Publicity of the wrong kind is never good for a company. Fires. Suicide. What's next?"

Yes, Carolyn wondered uneasily. *What's next?*

Adam was wondering the same thing as they returned to their suite. "I think I'd better work tonight," he told Carolyn as he shut the door behind them.

"Work? What do you mean?" She searched his face. Was he regretting the afternoon's lovemaking, finding an excuse not to go to bed with her tonight?

He must have read the question in her eyes, because he answered gently, "Darling, I'd much rather crawl into bed with you and hold you in my arms till morning."

"Then why…?"

He kissed her forehead. "Why the urgency? The longer my investigation takes, the greater number of people who'll be innocent victims. The only thing I'm sure of, is that someone is putting in bogus orders. It seemed reasonable that we have to be dealing with more than one person. Someone has to facilitate the orders and transport them illegally. By checking orders against shipments, I may be able to spot some discrepancies."

"But you can't go to Horizon at this time of night. Someone will surely tell Della, and she'll be suspicious."

"I know, which is why I've kept my hotel room. I have a computer there that can access private programs of the FDA, and I can e-mail them questions and clues for evaluation. I've already submitted some files I took off Arthur's computer and asked for a check of wholesale and retail businesses that place orders with Horizon."

"I guess there's nothing I can do to help you."

"No one is more essential to the success of this investigation than you are," he assured her lovingly. "Just keep playing your role, and we'll succeed."

She put her arms around his neck and raised her lips to his. "What role?"

He smiled and took a few minutes to show her.

WHEN HE SETTLED DOWN to work in his hotel room, Adam made a call to the agent who'd been staking out Cliff's apartment. The report was negative. No one had shown up by midnight when the stakeout ended.

Another disappointment was the analysis of the disks he'd sent to Angelica. Everything on Arthur's computer records checked out. There were no inconsistencies in orders, addresses and deliveries. They were all cleared as legitimate, no bogus orders or false company addresses on the list.

Angelica wasn't happy with the dead end when he called and told her. She was even less pleased when he told her about the fire and Susan Kimble's suicide. "Do you think the two are connected?" she asked.

"I haven't any evidence, but my gut says yes." He repeated the contents of the suicide note. "Sounds like a guilty conscience to me. Of course, it might be because she was pregnant and not have anything to do with her position as business manager."

"If your hunch is right and she was involved in handling the black-market orders, wouldn't her being out of the picture mean the illegal operation would shut down?"

"It might. Unless someone else is ready to take her place," he speculated.

"Then you better move fast on this."

"Yes, ma'am, I reckon as how I should," he replied in an exaggerated Texas drawl. "Thank y'all for reminding me."

His sarcasm wasn't lost on her, and her tone changed. "And how is the marriage going, cowboy?" she asked.

He hesitated a second too long.

"Adam?"

"It's working," he answered.

"You don't sound too sure."

"I'm always sure," he lied. As long as it didn't affect the investigation, it was really none of his boss's business what kind of relationship had developed between him and Carolyn. At the moment he wasn't quite certain how to deal with this wellspring of love that had burst in him. He only knew that Carolyn was the most precious thing in his life, and the responsibility of keeping her safe rested on him.

He worked until midnight, going over every known fact, every possible suspect and every aspect of recent events that could have a bearing on the case. As he laid out all the information, it became clear to him that Susan Kimble, as business manager, could've been in a pivotal position. Her suicide created a lot of questions that needed to be answered. What had laid so heavily on her conscience that she was willing to kill herself and her unborn child? Who was the father? Was her personal life separate from her position at Horizon? As Adam drove back to the mansion in the misty darkness, he mulled these questions over in his mind.

Carolyn was asleep when he quietly slipped into bed, but when he saw that she was lying in the middle, instead of on her usual side, he moved closer to her. Her warmth and the faint scent of her perfume sharpened his memory of their lovemaking, and he had to exert a lot of self-discipline not to touch her when she rolled over and snuggled against him. She murmured a sigh of contentment, but did not come fully awake. Her total acceptance of his physical closeness, as she lay next to him without fear and without reservation, was a balm to his soul. As he listened to her quiet breathing, he closed his eyes, and the day's events slid from his mind as he drifted into a contended sleep.

WHEN CAROLYN AWOKE in the morning, Adam was already dressed, and she could tell from the expression on his face that he had been waiting for her to stir.

"What is it?" she asked, sitting up and brushing back her hair. Satiated with yesterday's lovemaking, she'd slept well, but now, looking at Adam, she regretted that she hadn't awakened before he got out of bed. She glanced at the bedside clock.

"Only six-thirty? This early rising is getting to be a bad habit."

He sat down on the bed and kissed her sleep-flushed face. "I know it's early, and I wish we could spend the day here, but we can't. We have to get to Susan's office before anything gets moved or changed. I can't do it by myself without stepping out of my cover, but you can. It's your company and you have the right to examine anything you want to. We really ought to get in position before the Dragon Lady takes charge. That means we should leave now and catch some breakfast later." He smiled and kissed the tip of her nose. "Okay, my love?"

She savored the endearment as she nodded. "But I'm holding you to a promise to make it up later in the day. Give me ten minutes."

As she made her way to the bathroom, she felt his eyes on her and was grateful that Lisa had talked her into the silk gown that clung to her body and slithered when she moved. She didn't think she'd ever felt so happy. So at peace with herself. She'd given herself in almost total abandonment to love. Whatever happened, she would never again doubt that life could be beautiful, if only for a few hours.

WHEN THEY ENTERED THE business office at Horizon, it was empty of staff. No one occupied any of the cubicles or offices. Susan's office was at the back of the department and was a reflection of her personality. All the surfaces in her office were uncluttered, and the walls were bare except for calendars and public relation posters about Horizon. Her desk held the usual array of pens, notepads and filing baskets, but no personal pictures or mementos. When they opened the desk drawers, they found nothing of any consequence.

"She cleaned out everything," Carolyn said with a catch in her throat. "She knew what she was going to do. It wasn't a spur-of-the-moment thing."

"I'm afraid so." Adam eyed the computer. What were the chances she'd left anything incriminating on files or disks? Almost none. Everything about Susan's manner and appearance had radiated competency. Adam wondered how such a woman had allowed herself to get pregnant. Susan's emotions must have overridden her basic nature.

A quick search of the office verified what they already knew. Susan had cleaned house recently. "I need time to view her computer files. If I could take the computer to the hotel, I could do a better job. What do you think?"

She nodded. "I'll leave a note that I've taken it,

so no one will report a theft.'' Carolyn sighed. ''Della will have a fit. I'm afraid a showdown with her is coming before I'm ready.''

''You could be right,'' Adam agreed. The Dragon Lady had all her resources in place, and the minute Carolyn tried to exert her authority, she'd meet with fierce resistance. Adam just didn't know what the battle lines would include—corporate management or the illegal activity hidden within the company.

They put Susan's computer in the car, having satisfied security that the owner of the company was the one making off with it.

They decided to have a quick breakfast at the same restaurant they'd met Susan and Cliff that day at lunch. Carolyn couldn't get the dead woman out of her mind as they ate. Questions whirled like dry leaves in a windstorm. Was Cliff the father of the unborn child? Was he dallying with Lisa at the same time Susan was turning on the gas? Were both Cliff and Susan involved in the black-market scam?

Carolyn sighed as she pushed away her second cup of coffee. ''What's next?''

''I'd like to look over the packaging department and have a talk with Elinor. Hopefully she'll be able to tell us what were in those boxes that burned.''

''I doubt she'll be very cooperative if she's the one who set the fire,'' Carolyn countered flatly.

''Then we'll hope she trips herself up in some fashion.'' He gave Carolyn a reassuring smile. ''We have to treat everything she says as pieces in a puzzle. They'll all fit somewhere.'' He added silently, *And it better be soon!*

When they returned to Horizon, Elinor was busy

assessing the damage to the packing room; only one corner of the large department had been affected.

"It could have been worse," she admitted. "Most of the boxes ready to be moved to shipping were on the other side of the room. Once we get everything cleared out, we can give production the green light and slowly get everything back to normal."

"Do you have any idea what was in the boxes that were destroyed?" Adam asked.

She looked at him as if he'd just delivered a major insult. "Of course I know what was in them," she answered testily. "Do you think all the labeling and tracking we do is some parlor game?"

"You'll have to educate us, Elinor," Carolyn said quickly with an apologetic smile. "Do you stack the boxes in some order before they're moved to shipping?"

"Not all of them, but controlled substances and experimental drugs are kept on this side of the room. The orders are checked twice before they leave this department."

"And the boxes that were destroyed, what was in them?" Adam prodded.

"They contained a drug, a new antibiotic Horizon hopes to market that's being tested for FDA approval by Eventide Research, Inc. They're conducting a three-year study to determine if there are any health risks."

Adam's mind raced. *Experimental drug. Was this the unapproved antibiotic that had killed Marietta?*

If Elinor truly was innocent, he speculated that only legitimate orders were being packaged for delivery to Eventide Research, Inc. Someone there would have complained if their orders were not being fully filled.

"That's a reputable research center," Carolyn said thoughtfully. "I know they have several different programs and the hospital made quite a few referrals to them." She frowned. "But I don't understand why anyone would want to set fire to their orders."

Elinor shrugged. "Lots of crazies in the world."

"Any ideas?" Adam prodded.

She shrugged. "I tend to my own business."

The way she said it made Adam think that it was not necessarily true. This brisk, no-nonsense woman was in exactly the right place to know if bogus orders were coming through the packaging and production departments. She was also in a pivotal position between the packaging and shipping departments. He decided to ask her exactly what he needed to know.

"Elinor, how could extra boxes of experimental drugs get through Horizon's carefully monitored procedures?"

"They couldn't," Elinor said flatly. "Too many checks and balances. Every labeled drug has to have a legitimate order number, and every shipment has an address that matches the invoice. At least six people have to sign off on every order."

Carolyn's chest tightened.

Could Adam be wrong about Horizon's involvement? Was he on a misguided crusade?

As they left the packaging department, Carolyn said, "I feel like having a talk with my dear uncle this morning. Alone."

"I think that's a good idea," Adam answered.

"You know your way around a laboratory, and you have every right to ask all the questions you want."

Carolyn didn't tell him that the questions she wanted to ask her uncle were of a personal nature. It infuriated her that Jasper was so closedmouthed about Alicia. Most siblings would have had some childhood memories about the family to share, but not Jasper; all he had were a few snapshots of himself, and he'd deliberately avoided any mention of his sister or his own father when talking to Carolyn. The frustration and disappointment of her attic search firmed her steps as she made her way upstairs.

Jasper was in his office. She could see through the windowed wall that he was sitting at his desk, poring over some papers. She gave a polite knock on the door and without waiting for an invitation to enter, opened it and went in.

He looked startled, and the beginning of a frown deepened the lines on his forehead. Then he seemed to catch himself as he stood up. "Carolyn. We missed you at breakfast this morning."

His tone had the edge of a reprimand, which Carolyn ignored. She wasn't going to be treated like a child who had to account for her whereabouts.

"I'd like to talk to you for a few minutes, Uncle Jasper, if you have the time." She didn't wait for his reply, but sat down in a chair at the side of his desk.

"Yes, of course." He hesitated for a moment as if reluctant to sit back down. "If you'd like to look over the lab—"

"No, not right now," she answered firmly. "I have some personal questions that need answering."

The tone of her voice must have warned him because he visibly stiffened. "I'm not sure I can supply the kind of information you're seeking."

"You're the only one who can tell me why you seem to hate even the mention of my mother," she said bluntly.

He stared at her for a moment as if about to deny it. Then he sat, clasped his hands on the desk and said wearily, "So it shows, does it?"

"Can you tell me why?"

He stared at his clasped hands. "I can't remember the first time I realized I disliked my sister intensely. I think it was the Christmas Alicia was four. There were all kinds of exciting presents for her under the tree, and all I was given was a set of serviceable new winter clothes. When I tried to play with some of her toys, I was made fun of." His eyes hardened. "My parents really only had one child—Alicia. They gave their daughter all their attention and love. Unfortunately they neglected to teach her anything about responsibility. And she broke their hearts."

He leaned back in his chair. "After she died, my father focused all his energy on business. He ignored my mother and me, and when she died, he just had me to shut out of his life."

Carolyn wanted to go around the desk and put a consoling hand on his shoulder, as if the contact might help make things up for the lonely boy who was never loved. In a way he had lived the same kind of lonely life as she had.

"I tried in every way to make my father proud of me. I thought if I succeeded in business, he'd accept me." Jasper issued a bitter laugh. "All I did was prove that I didn't have his business sense and was exactly the failure he'd thought. Then he found you, his daughter's child, and gave you all of this." He waved his hand. "Funny how the past repeats itself, isn't it?"

The way Jasper looked at Carolyn told her the hatred he'd felt for her mother had been transferred to her. She had a sickening feeling that Jasper was capable of the treachery that could have killed Arthur Stanford and set Horizon's black-market trade in motion.

Chapter Fifteen

Adam's determination to find a discrepancy in Susan's records kept him working in his hotel room way into the night.

Finally, exasperated, he called Angelica. "There's absolutely no record of any orders going to a company that is not approved for testing new drugs. I've checked and double-checked her records and computer files. It doesn't seem reasonable that she could have left a completely clean operation that involves so many people and departments. Someone is initiating orders that are going to the black market, but I haven't a clue who and how."

"You'd better bring what you have and come to D.C. Sometimes a fresh eye helps. Take a red-eye flight out tonight. I'll expect you at the safe house tomorrow."

He opened his mouth to protest, but changed his mind. Angelica could be right. Maybe he was overlooking something obvious.

Adam called Carolyn from his hotel, and woke her up to tell her that he had to make a quick trip to D.C. "I have to report to my superiors. I'll leave the hotel in a few minutes and go straight to the airport.''

"But it's the middle of the night," she protested as she peered at the clock.

"I know, but I can get a red-eye to D.C. I'll grab the few things I have here in the hotel room and buy whatever else I need.''

"How long will you be gone?"

"A couple of days at most," he assured her with more confidence that he felt. "You have to promise me something. While I'm away, you need to pretend you're not feeling well and stay away from the office.''

"Why?"

"Because I don't know what in hell is going on. You could stumble onto something without even knowing it. And don't leave the house—for any reason! Are you listening to me?''

She mumbled something.

"Sweetheart, promise me you'll do what I say." He softened his voice. "I love you. How can I do my job if I spend my time worrying about you?"

"Why do you have to go without me?" she protested. "We're in this together and—"

"Carolyn, you can't go with me," he said firmly. "I'll call you. Trust me on this, and do as I say."

He could tell she wasn't convinced, and after he hung up, he wondered if she'd do as he ordered. She could be as stubborn as any woman he'd known, and he had an uneasy feeling that he should cancel his trip and make sure she stayed safe.

CAROLYN HAD TROUBLE getting back to sleep. She could tell from Adam's voice that he was uptight, worried about leaving her and less than pleased about having to fly to D.C. Sighing, she turned over in bed and hugged his pillow. Maybe his superiors would find the answers they'd been looking for. She hoped, more than anything, that they could get on with their lives without the constant threat of danger hanging over them.

She was surprised when Adam called her again the next morning and exacted another promise from her that she wouldn't go to the office until he got back. This time she didn't argue. Their separation seemed to crystallize the deep feelings they'd developed for each other.

After she hung up, she realized that she was glad to have some leisure time. She couldn't remember when there'd been no demands, no obligations and no one in authority breathing down her neck.

She dressed comfortably in jeans and a T-shirt, and spent the day going over company reports, eating and wandering around the estate grounds. Mack seemed more than willing to have her in his greenhouse, and she gave in to the temptation to swim in the heated pool. Everything she did during the day seemed to remind her how much she wished Adam was there with her. She missed his smile, his intense gray blue eyes and his tender touch.

She was waiting for his call when he phoned her at about eight that evening.

"I'm planning on taking a flight back tomorrow afternoon," he told her. "There's nothing more we can do here. We've looked at everything in depth and haven't found the answers. Our next step will be placing one of our people in every area of Horizon's operation. That's where you come in, honey.

You'll have to take charge and do the firing and hiring so we get everyone in the right place.''

She groaned. ''I can't think of anything I'd hate more. Della will throw a fit if I start interfering with personnel.''

''There's no other way. Besides, you have to start taking control sometime, don't you? Your grandfather put you in a position of authority. He could have left Della fifty-one of the company, instead of you,'' he reminded her.

''In some ways I wish he had.''

''Hey, that isn't the Carolyn I know,'' he chided.

''Maybe you don't know me all that well.''

''Oh, yes, I do,'' he said. ''When it comes to your courage, determination and loyalty, I'd stake my life on it—in fact, I have.''

The tone of their conversation changed, and they began to share their feelings for each other. Their forced separation made it clear they'd fallen deeply in love.

After Carolyn hung up the phone, she was too restless to read or think about going to bed. Buddy and Lisa were out as usual, and so were Della and Jasper, who were attending a college lecture that had interested Jasper.

When Carolyn heard a car pull into the garage, she glanced at her watch. Only nine o'clock. The lecture must have ended early.

Carolyn decided that there was no time like the present to face the Dragon Lady. Della had told her that she usually worked a couple of hours in her home office every night before retiring. Maybe dropping a few hints about her intention to review the staff might prepare Della for the changes Adam wanted her to make, Carolyn thought hopefully. She'd rather have the scene here at the house than at the office.

Bracing herself for an unpleasant confrontation, Carolyn made her way to the other wing of the house. She'd been in Della's office once before and was relieved that the door was open and the lights were on.

Taking a deep breath, she walked into the room. She expected to see Della at her desk, but it was Buddy who was sitting in front of the computer, his back to the door. Probably playing a computer game, she thought. Wasting his time as usual.

As she walked up behind him and quietly looked over his shoulder, a teasing remark died on her lips. He wasn't engrossed in a computer game. On the monitor was a sophisticated software program that made little sense to her, with her limited knowledge of software.

Before she could say anything, he acknowledged her presence.

"Hello, Carolyn. Your sweet perfume gives you away." He swung around to face her, and at the same time reached into an open leather bag on the desk beside him. "I'm really sorry about this." In a split second he had a gun pointed at her.

She stared at him in disbelief. The truth hit her with the devastating force of an avalanche. "It's you!"

"Yep, it's me, all right. Good for nothing Buddy. Playing a game as usual." He gave her his happy-go-lucky grin. "Only this time it's a game with a real payoff. A game that I'm winning and you're about to lose, Carolyn. Who would have thought it?''

Swallowing hard, she echoed, ''Yes, who would have thought it? But how…?''

''How did I pull it off?'' Buddy gave a satisfied chuckle as he kept his gun leveled at her. ''How did I run my black-market scheme right under everyone's noses and no one saw it? Easy. Everybody trusted the numbers the computer reported because they looked fine. And why not? The computer program that controls the entire production process at Horizon is an amazing piece of software. Everything that happens in the entire production process from start to finish is reported. But the numbers the computer reported were wrong. I ran extra orders through the process that were never reported.''

Even Carolyn's limited knowledge made such a cover-up seem virtually impossible. ''How?''

''How did I defeat the security and audit trails built into the production software? I guess you deserve to know now that the game is over, but first I have to make certain that this little talk remains between you and me. You and your nosy husband didn't fool me for a minute.'' He shook his curly head. ''Too bad. Now I've got to make things a little messy for all of us. You and I have to take a little trip in my boat.''

''You can't get away with something like this.'' She spoke as firmly as she could, with her mouth and throat as parched as a desert. She glanced at the closed door between the office and the bedroom.

''They're not home. I just got here myself, so we have the house all to ourselves.''

She knew then that it wasn't Della and Jasper

she'd heard returning to the house, but Buddy. "I'll scream and the servants will come," she warned.

He shrugged. "Then I'll just have to shoot them, too." The calm delivery of this statement told her he would do exactly that.

Checkmate, she thought with a lurch of panic. He had bought her silence more effectively than a gag in her mouth. How could she willingly endanger the lives of others to save herself? She couldn't, and he must have known it.

He motioned with the gun. "We're going to walk down the back hall, nice and easy. There's a stairway that will take us to the first floor and a side door."

She remembered that Adam had taken the servants' stairs down from this floor on that first day and had circled the house without anyone seeing him. Nothing Adam had said offered her any hope that someone would see Buddy holding a gun to her back as they made their way out of the house in the darkness and down to his boat.

They moved along the hall, past Lisa's empty bedroom. Apparently she was out for the evening or the night. Carolyn wondered if she was with Cliff or someone else. Did she have any idea of the masquerade her brother had played?

When they reached the boat dock, Buddy forced her down a couple of steps into the small cabin cruiser, then shoved her roughly down on a small bed and grabbed a nearby coil of rope. She swallowed back a swell of hysteria as Buddy secured her ankles and wrists with it. He was deaf to her pleas and handled her with frightening detachment.

When he seemed satisfied she wasn't going anywhere, he straightened and said with a mocking grin, "Welcome to my home away from home."

As if he'd been waiting a long time to have someone appreciate him, he began to brag about how he'd been able to run a black-market scam right under their noses.

"See these books?" He unlocked a cupboard and waved at stacks of computer books and software. "When everyone thought I was out fishing or loafing, I was learning and studying everything I could about computers and the programs that run on them. I'm what you call a gifted nerd," he boasted.

Desperately Carolyn hoped that if she could keep him talking long enough, someone in the house might notice that the lights were on in his boat and come to investigate. "You certainly fooled everyone."

"People are stupid," he answered flatly.

"You must really be a genius to be able to completely hide what you're doing." She fought the tremor in her voice. "How did you manage?"

"While Mom was at work, I went through all the programs on her home computer that are being used throughout the company." He gave Carolyn a superior smile. "I decided that, instead of tampering with the programs that track the entire drug production from start to shipping, I'd come in the back door, so to speak, and develop my own."

"Back door?" Carolyn echoed, trying to make sense of what he was saying on one level of her mind, while grasping for some way to save herself on another.

"Horizon has an 'integrated production tracking system.' All the information stored in a computer is controlled by the DBMS. Oh, I forgot, you're not computer literate,'' he said impatiently. ''DBMS stands for Database Management System, and I needed a password to access this system.'' He chuckled. ''Mom changes the password all the time, and she has to keep writing it down so she won't forget—that's how I know what it is. With this password I've been able to log in as the database administrator and make any changes I want.''

Fear battled her insides as Carolyn struggled to focus on what he was saying. She was sure now he'd been responsible for her grandfather's death and would eliminate her, too, without a qualm. Keeping him talking was about the only weapon she had to delay whatever he planned to do with her.

''And you came in the back door how, Buddy?'' She tried to maintain a pose of interest.

''With my own programs to manipulate the data files, I could enter as many hidden orders as I wanted. When the system finished processing these orders, all references to them were deleted. As far as Horizon's computer records show, they never existed.''

''You couldn't have gotten them through the whole system without help. Susan knew about the false orders, didn't she?''

He gave her his boyish grin. ''Very good, Carolyn. If someone were to run a report while bogus orders were being processed, there would be a paper record that might alert someone to my scheme. That's where Susan came in. She had to make sure that didn't happen. She was very good. Printers jammed, ran out of toner, ran out of paper, or they lost their network connection. Everyone accepted all the printer troubles and missing reports as being normal. And since the reports just had to be rerun, it wasn't seen as a problem. Susan was a good gal.''

''And she killed herself because she couldn't go on with the deception.''

''Susan was a perfect accomplice—until she got a touch of conscience. Trying to burn the latest batch of orders was pure stupidity. Now, I have to close down sooner than I planned.''

''How did you get her to agree in the first place?'' Even as Carolyn voiced the question, she knew the answer. He'd been her lover. Buddy had played on the unattractive young woman's emotions and used her for his own gain. His callousness was chilling. ''You're the father of her unborn child, aren't you?''

''An unexpected complication,'' he admitted with a shrug. ''You wouldn't expect a smart girl like Susan to get herself in a jam like that, would you?''

Carolyn couldn't disguise her disgust as she glared at him. ''How can you live with yourself?''

''Easy. I've got enough money to live the good life in any country that suits my fancy.''

''Who else is involved in this despicable scam of yours?''

His expression hardened as he avoided a direct answer. ''Just a few more loose ends to take care of.''

Her heart seemed to lurch to a stop. The way he looked at her, she knew that she was one of those loose ends.

''What are you going to do with me?''

''Carolyn, honey, you're going to take a little sea voyage. I've got a nice boat coming in for a rendezvous to pick up some merchandise. I'll pay the captain to take you out to sea and drop you overboard. No body. No evidence.'' He grinned as if pleased at how clever he was.

Chuckling, he left her in the cabin and started the engine. He eased the small cruiser away from the dock and soon it disappeared into the night.

Chapter Sixteen

In the morning, Adam called Carolyn from the D.C. airport to tell her he was coming in earlier than expected. When she didn't answer the private phone in their study, he decided she must be somewhere else in the house—or she'd ignored his warning and gone somewhere. He was tempted to call Horizon and see if she was there, but decided he'd have it out with her in a few hours when he was back in Seattle.

He called her again after he'd landed, but still no answer. Where was she? He dialed the house number and talked to Morna.

"I haven't seen her this morning," the housekeeper replied crisply. "But then, she never tells me what to expect. Sometimes it's breakfast, no lunch and maybe dinner for the two of you. How am I supposed to give orders to the cook?" she complained.

"We'll have to work that out," Adam answered, holding back his impatience. "Will you check and see if Carolyn is still in our suite? I'll hold."

She surely wouldn't be sleeping through the noon hour, he thought, especially if she missed breakfast.

Unless she was sick? He waited anxiously for Morna to come back on the line.

"She's not there," the housekeeper told him after what seemed like an eternity. "She must have left the house early, even before Della and Jasper."

Adam swore as he hung up. Now he was sure she'd ignored his warnings to stay away from Horizon until he got back. She must have decided to do some investigating on her own.

He dialed her office number, but she didn't answer, and then he called Della. She informed him that she hadn't seen Carolyn since the night before when they left the house to attend a lecture.

"Was her car in the garage when you left this morning?"

Della thought for a moment. "Yes, I believe it was. Okay, if Carolyn's not at the house, someone must have picked her up for a day's outing. One of her old friends, perhaps." Her tone suggested slyly that it could have been a man.

"Maybe Carolyn went shopping with Lisa in her car," Adam said.

"I doubt it," Della answered curtly. "My daughter has chosen to spend her time elsewhere these days."

Adam hurriedly engaged a taxi, and on the way to the mansion, he tried to figure out why Carolyn wouldn't have taken her new car if she was going out with someone like Rosie. It didn't make sense. Where had she gone? And who with? Maybe she'd left a note, he thought hopefully.

He let himself into the house and bounded up the stairs. When he reached their suite of rooms, he was struck by several disquieting discoveries.

No note. He could see that Carolyn hadn't spent the night there. The bed was turned down, but it hadn't been slept in. Her nightgown and robe were hanging on a hook in the bathroom. A book lay open on the couch, and when he'd called her the evening before she'd been reading.

A vice tightened in his chest. Experience had taught him not to give way to his emotions. Nothing was gained by falling apart when a clear head was needed. As he walked slowly through each room, he forced himself to examine the situation rationally.

No sign of any struggle.

Opening the drawer where she kept her purse, he saw it was still there. As far as he could tell none of her coats or jackets were missing from the closet. What would cause her to leave with someone in such a hurry that she would have left these behind?

A telephone call?

An emergency?

He raced downstairs to the kitchen and questioned Seika, Lotuse and their father. Adam was aware that servants often knew more about what went on in a household than anyone else. They all shook their heads. None of them had seen her since dinner the night before. Adam left the house, circled the grounds looking for Mack and found him pruning the rose garden.

"Haven't seen her today," the gardener said, wiping his sweaty forehead. "Yesterday she was enjoying the greenhouse and grounds. Nice lady. Got a good feel for plants, too. It's nice to have someone around who appreciates nature's beauty." He lowered his voice. "Not like the rest of the women in the house."

Adam was on his way back to the house when he saw Buddy's white cruiser pulling into the dock. As Adam approached the boat, Buddy greeted him with a wave and showed off a string of fish he had in his hand.

"Got some beauties here. You ought to join me sometime, Adam. Nothing like a good morning's catch to set the world right."

"Have you seen Carolyn today?" Adam asked.

"Nope." He shook his curly head. "But I pulled out about four o'clock this morning. Too early for most people."

"What about Lisa? Have you seen her today?"

"Naw. She didn't come home. I think she's shacking up with some guy. Mom's pretty steamed about it, too."

Adam didn't want to get sidetracked into a discussion of his sister's behavior. "When was the last time you saw Carolyn?"

"At dinner," Buddy answered readily. "She said she was tired and was going to turn in early. I did get the impression, though, that she had something on her mind to do today."

Or last night? Adam added silently. *But what?*

When night fell and still no sign of her, Adam called the police and reported her missing. He used his influence to get the authorities on the case. They searched the grounds, looking for footprints, but there was no sign of an intruder.

Had she been kidnapped? As the night wore on,

Adam's attention began to center on the two suspects who might need money badly enough to try to extort money for Carolyn's safety.

Cliff was first on the list. Nick was second.

Adam drove to Cliff's apartment and woke up Cliff and Lisa. He grilled them about Carolyn's disappearance and was satisfied that their alibis held up.

Nick's place was located in Port Townsend, and Adam had to take a ferry to get there. The homes were old, and Nick's looked as if it had weathered many a storm. A faint light showed in one of the front windows, and the steps creaked as Adam mounted them to the front door. He was about to knock on the scarred wooden door when he realized it was ajar.

"Nick," he called as he poked his head into a small hallway with an opening on each side. "Nick, it's Adam. You here?"

He waited, no answer. A gut feeling made him draw his gun. If Nick had Carolyn a prisoner in the house, he'd need it. He listened for any betraying sound. But there was nothing. No squeaking floorboards, no muffled footsteps. Nothing.

As he moved cautiously to the living room doorway, he saw why. Nick lay in a pool of blood. Shot through the heart. Carolyn! Was she involved in some way?

With his gun poised and ready to shoot, he made his way through the small house, but found nothing to indicate she'd been there. Nor did he find anything to identify who had entered Nick's house and killed him. If the demand had been for a gambling debt, Nick had paid in full—with his life.

Adam knelt over Nick's body, which was still warm. As he emptied the man's pockets, he was disappointed to find the usual things: keys, wallet with a little money in it, some antacid tablets. He almost missed a crumpled piece of paper that was stuffed in Nick's shirt pocket. A printed shipping label. The company name on it didn't match any of those that had been on Horizon's computers, Adam was sure of it. As he stared at the address, it tugged at a memory. He turned it over in his mind and then he remembered. The address was in the same waterfront area where Carolyn's grandfather was run over. Had Arthur Stanford discovered something similar, like this shipping label, that took him to that area? Adam's thoughts raced. Had Carolyn stumbled into something as perilous?

Adam called 911, reported Nick's murder, then drove to an area that had streets bordering clusters of marinas, warehouses and waterfront businesses. Peering at indistinct signs, Adam finally determined that he was several blocks from where Arthur was killed. The address on the crumpled shipping label belonged to a dark, three-story building, and boat dock.

Was Arthur heading here when something made him get out of his car and then he was deliberately run over?

In Nick's position as head of the shipping department, he could have diverted orders by covering up the name of a legitimate company and address with a label that sent the shipment to *this* address. Adam parked a half block from the warehouse and approached the building from the side. As he reached a narrow parking area that led to the wharf and boat dock, Adam recognized the lone car parked there. It was Buddy's.

Before he could give meaning to this discovery, he heard muffled noises. Above the sucking and lapping sound of water, he recognized Carolyn's weak cry somewhere ahead on the shadowy wharf.

Adam hugged the side of the building as he ran forward and peered around the corner. He saw two shadowy figures come out the back door and he recognized them both.

CAROLYN WHIMPERED as Buddy roughly pushed her forward, holding one arm behind her back in a painful position. Dizzy from some pills Buddy had forced on her, and stiff from her cramped confinement in a small storage closet, she stumbled.

Buddy had taunted her that she'd be the first cargo loaded when the foreign ship pulled in. Her hopes had faded that somehow, some way, Adam would find her, and she thought she was hallucinating when she heard his voice.

"Let her go, Buddy," Adam ordered as he stepped out into the dim light of a high arc light. "Now! Or I'll shoot."

Buddy swung around, clutching Carolyn in front of him like a shield. When he saw it was Adam, he grinned and taunted, "Go ahead. Save me the trouble of shipping her out."

"You're under arrest, Buddy. Now we'll add kidnapping to your other crimes, like murder."

"Oh, so you found poor old Nick," Buddy said, almost as if he was pleased to take credit for the crime. "Sorry to disappoint you, but there has to be a loser in any game. In this one it's you!"

"Behind you!" Carolyn croaked.

The waterfront thug Buddy had hired to be her jailor jumped Adam and knocked the gun from his hand. The revolver fell into the water.

Adam had spent hours training in martial arts and now put the training to good use. He landed a knockout blow to his attacker's chin and instantly dropped the man to the splintered boards of the wharf.

As Buddy tried to reach for his gun, he lost his grip on Carolyn. Twisting free, she clawed at his face with her fingernails. Swearing, he tried to get free of her. As he knocked her away, Adam threw himself at Buddy with a fierce tackle that sent them both reeling backward.

Exchanging blows, they rolled, wrestled and moved closer and closer to the edge of the wharf. Suddenly, locked in a deadly grip, they disappeared over the side.

Carolyn screamed and searched the dark waters lapping the weathered piles. No sign of them. Terrified and sobbing, she struggled to her feet and stumbled up and down the wharf. She peered into the murky depths.

"Adam! Adam!"

No answer. Then a sudden movement a short distance down the wharf brought a rush of adrenaline through her. Who had made it out of the water?

Her heart stopped. Her breath quickened. And then joyful air filled her lungs. The figure that had pulled himself up on the wharf was Adam.

She staggered toward him and when she reached him, fell into his wet arms as if she'd never let him go.

A hurried call on Adam's cell phone brought the authorities to the wharf. After a thorough search, they located a dazed Buddy clinging to a weathered pile.

The deadly game was over.

Adam tightened the arm he had around her and said, "Let's go home, my darling."

Chapter Seventeen

After the police cars had left, Adam wanted to take Carolyn to the hospital to make sure she was all right, but she refused.

"Please, just take me home," she pleaded in a tremulous voice.

They looked like fugitives from a war zone as they made their way to his car. Her steps were unsteady as she leaned against him for support, her hair a tangled mess, her face smudged and pallid. Water dripped from his clothes and his drenched hair.

They sat close together in the car seat, blessing the warmth of the car heater as Adam drove back to the mansion. He told Carolyn about Nick's murder and his conviction that Arthur had somehow learned about the warehouse address and was checking it out when Buddy hit him with his car. Carolyn filled him in on the discovery she'd made about Buddy and the way he'd used his mother's computer and password to enter and delete false orders.

Adam let out a slow whistle. "What a waste of a brilliant mind. If Buddy had put all that creativity into a legitimate endeavor, he could have made himself a lot more money in the long run."

"And Susan and Nick might still be alive."

"I'm sure that Susan's affection for Buddy was the motivation for her willingness to do what he wanted. Then, when she got pregnant, she realized the truth and tried to burn the boxes that were slated for the black market."

"And poor Nick." Carolyn shook her head. "He was getting it from two directions."

Adam nodded. "Nick needed money so badly for his gambling debts that he agreed to switch the shipping labels on the extra orders."

"Only to get killed when Buddy didn't need his help anymore. It all makes sense now, doesn't it." Carolyn sighed. "Why couldn't we see it before?"

"That's the way it is with a puzzle. Once you put in the last piece, you see the whole picture."

Leaning her head back in the seat, she closed her eyes. "So it's really over?"

He knew what she was asking.

Where do we go from here?

The way was clear now for her to accept the responsibilities her inheritance had thrust on her. She was free to take over the reins at Horizon and prove her capabilities. The unwanted changeling would emerge as a young woman who had it all—money, power and prestige.

"Yes, it's really over," he said with a catch in his throat.

They both fell silent.

EVEN THOUGH THEY TRIED to hold on to the passionate feelings that remained between them, the demands made on both of them began to intrude as the weeks passed. Adam was involved in tying all the ends of his investigation together and working with the authorities to bring a satisfactory end to the case. He was in D.C. a lot of the time, and the relationship between him and Carolyn started to become a long-distance one.

Carolyn learned that Adam had taken his first and middle names, Adam Lawrence, for his undercover, but his real last name was Anderson. *Mrs. Adam Anderson.* The name held no familiarity and seemed to be a symbol of the growing distance between them.

Della and Jasper had been shaken by Buddy's deception, and they made unexpected overtures to Carolyn at home and at work. Della was devastated by what her son had done and was willing to make up for his criminal activity in any way she could. As Della spent hours with her, instructing her in detailed workings of the company, Carolyn could see why her grandfather had placed such confidence in Della's ability.

Jasper's overtures to Carolyn invited a different relationship between them. It was as if he'd shed some of his deep resentments from the past and was ready to view what had happened in a different light. Even Lisa seemed willing to listen to Carolyn's concerned warnings about her involvement with Cliff.

Even though Buddy's treachery had left some good in its wake, Carolyn viewed her new future with a sense of deep loss.

ADAM TRIED TO compensate for the gulf developing between him and Carolyn by burying himself in the agency in Washington, D.C. They talked hours on the phone each week, but more and more the conversation centered on activities that weren't shared by the other. It was obvious to Adam that Carolyn was meeting new people, accepting new business challenges and getting oriented in an affluent social society. She hadn't officially taken over the reins of Horizon yet, but he expected an announcement any day.

He was concerned about the personal issues between them that had to be resolved, such as a legal annulment of their not-so-pretend marriage. The sooner the better, he thought, and as he booked a flight to Seattle, mentally rehearsed how best to handle the emotional breakup.

Carolyn was waiting for him in their suite when he arrived, and he groaned when he saw her. She was wearing the red silk dress that teased him with every touch and kiss he'd placed on her luscious body. He'd never thought of her as a temptress, but as she slowly walked toward him, he knew he'd be lost if he gave in to the inviting smile on her lips.

"We need to talk," he said quickly, keeping his arms at his side, instead of reaching for her as his heart commanded.

She nodded, still smiling. "Yes, I feel like a tight-rope walker about to fall without a safety net. I want to make sure you're there to catch me."

"You're not going to fall, Carolyn," he said firmly. Her words and smile only heightened the pain of ending their intimate relationship. "You're going to be a wonderful success in the business world, and you know it. You have everything it takes to succeed at anything you put your mind to."

She moved so close to him that the scent of her perfume teased his nostrils. "I'm glad to hear you say that, because I've made a decision. I don't want to be a success in the business world. I never did. I want to be a doctor. The best doctor in Washington, D.C.''

For a second his mind went blank. This conversation was not going at all the way he'd played it out in his mind. ''What are you saying?''

She touched his cheek with her fingertips. ''Simple, darling. I'm leaving Horizon in Della and Jasper's hands, and I'm moving with my husband to D.C. I'm ready to be Mrs. Adam Lawrence Anderson, or whatever your name happens to be at the moment.''

His mouth eased into a smile as he took her in his arms, and the kiss he gave her verified his whole-hearted acceptance and approval.

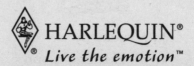

Is your man too good to be true?

Hot, gorgeous AND romantic?
If so, he could be a Harlequin® Blaze™ series cover model!

Our grand-prize winners will receive a trip for two to New York City to
shoot the cover of a Blaze novel, and will stay at the luxurious Plaza Hotel.
Plus, they'll receive $500 U.S. spending money!
The runner-up winners will receive $200 U.S.
to spend on a romantic dinner for two.

It's easy to enter!

In 100 words or less, tell us what makes your boyfriend or spouse a true romantic
and the perfect candidate for the cover of a Blaze novel, and include in your submission
two photos of this potential cover model.

All entries must include the written submission of the contest entrant, two photographs of the model
candidate and the Official Entry Form and Publicity Release forms completed in full and signed by
both the model candidate and the contest entrant. Harlequin, along with the experts at
Elite Model Management, will select a winner.

For photo and complete Contest details, please refer to the Official Rules on the next page. All entries
will become the property of Harlequin Enterprises Ltd. and are not returnable.

**Please visit www.blazecovermodel.com to download a copy of the Official Entry Form and
Publicity Release Form or send a request to one of the addresses below.**

Please mail your entry to: **Harlequin Blaze Cover Model Search**

In U.S.A.	In Canada
P.O. Box 9069	P.O. Box 637
Buffalo, NY	Fort Erie, ON
14269-9069	L2A 5X3

No purchase necessary. Contest open to Canadian and U.S. residents who are 18 and over.
Void where prohibited. Contest closes September 30, 2003.

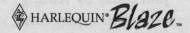

HBCVRMOD

HARLEQUIN BLAZE COVER MODEL SEARCH CONTEST 3569 OFFICIAL RULES
NO PURCHASE NECESSARY TO ENTER

. To enter, submit two (2) 4" x 6" photographs of a boyfriend or spouse (who must be 18 years of age or older) taken o later than three (3) months from the time of entry: a close-up, waist up, shirtless photograph; and a fully clothed, ull-length photograph, then, tell us, in 100 words or fewer, why he should be a Harlequin Blaze cover model and how e is romantic. Your complete "entry" must include: (i) your essay, (ii) the Official Entry Form and Publicity Release orm printed below completed and signed by you (as "Entrant"), (iii) the photographs (with your hand-written name, ddress and phone number, and your model's name, address and phone number on the back of each photograph), and v) the Publicity Release Form and Photograph Representation Form printed below completed and signed by your nodel (as "Model"), and should be sent via first-class mail to either: Harlequin Blaze Cover Model Search Contest 569, P.O. Box 9069, Buffalo, NY, 14269-9069, or Harlequin Blaze Cover Model Search Contest 3569, P.O. Box 637, ort Erie, Ontario L2A 5X3. All submissions must be in English and be received no later than September 30, 2003. imit: one entry per person, household or organization. **Purchase or acceptance of a product offer does not improve your hances of winning.** All entry requirements must be strictly adhered to for eligibility and to ensure fairness among entries.

. Ten (10) Finalist submissions (photographs and essays) will be selected by a panel of judges consisting of members f the Harlequin editorial, marketing and public relations staff, as well as a representative from Elite Model 1anagement (Toronto) Inc., based on the following criteria:

.ptness/Appropriateness of submitted photographs for a Harlequin Blaze cover—70%
.riginality of Essay—20%
incerity of Essay—10%

n the event of a tie, duplicate finalists will be selected. The photographs submitted by finalists will be posted on the 1arlequin website no later than November 15, 2003 (at www.blazecovermodel.com), and viewers may vote, in rank rder, on their favorite(s) to assist in the panel of judges' final determination of the Grand Prize and Runner-up winning ntries based on the above judging criteria. All decisions of the judges are final.

All entries become the property of Harlequin Enterprises Ltd. and none will be returned. Any entry may be used for ture promotional purposes. Elite Model Management (Toronto) Inc. and/or its partners, subsidiaries and affiliates perating as "Elite Model Management" will have access to all entries including all personal information, and may ontact any Entrant and/or Model in its sole discretion for their own business purposes. Harlequin and Elite Model 1anagement (Toronto) Inc. are separate entities with no legal association or partnership whatsoever having no power bind or obligate the other or create any expressed or implied obligation or responsibility on behalf of the other, such at Harlequin shall not be responsible in any way for any acts or omissions of Elite Model Management (Toronto) Inc. its partners, subsidiaries and affiliates in connection with the Contest or otherwise and Elite Model Management shall ot be responsible in any way for any acts or omissions of Harlequin or its partners, subsidiaries and affiliates in onnection with the contest or otherwise.

All Entrants and Models must be residents of the U.S. or Canada, be 18 years of age or older, and have no prior iminal convictions. The contest is not open to any Model that is a professional model and/or actor in any capacity at e time of the entry. Contest void wherever prohibited by law; all applicable laws and regulations apply. Any litigation ithin the Province of Quebec regarding the conduct or organization of a publicity contest may be submitted to the Régie es alcools, des courses et des jeux for a ruling, and any litigation regarding the awarding of a prize may be submitted the Régie only for the purpose of helping the parties reach a settlement. Employees and immediate family members Harlequin Enterprises Ltd., D.L. Blair, Inc., Elite Model Management (Toronto) Inc. and their parents, affiliates, bsidiaries and all other agencies, entities and persons connected with the use, marketing or conduct of this Contest are ot eligible to enter. Acceptance of any prize offered constitutes permission to use Entrants' and Models' names, essay bmissions, photographs or other likenesses for the purposes of advertising, trade, publication and promotion on behalf Harlequin Enterprises Ltd., its parent, affiliates, subsidiaries, assigns and other authorized entities involved in the dging and promotion of the contest without further compensation to any Entrant or Model, unless prohibited by law.

Finalists will be determined no later than October 30, 2003. Prize Winners will be determined no later than January , 2004. Grand Prize Winners (consisting of winning Entrant and Model) will be required to sign and return Affidavit Eligibility/Release of Liability and Model Release forms within thirty (30) days of notification. Non-compliance th this requirement and within the specified time period will result in disqualification and an alternate will be lected. Any prize notification returned as undeliverable will result in the awarding of the prize to an alternate set of nners. All travelers (or parent/legal guardian of a minor) must execute the Affidavit of Eligibility/Release of Liability ior to ticketing and must possess valid travel documents (e.g. valid photo ID) where applicable. Travel dates ecified by Sponsor but no later than May 30, 2004.

Prizes: One (1) Grand Prize—the opportunity for the Model to appear on the cover of a paperback book from the arlequin Blaze series, and a 3 day/2 night trip for two (Entrant and Model) to New York, NY for the photo shoot of odel which includes round-trip coach air transportation from the commercial airport nearest the winning Entrant's me to New York, NY, (or, in lieu of air transportation, $100 cash payable to Entrant and Model, if the winning Entrant's me is within 250 miles of New York, NY), hotel accommodations (double occupancy) at the Plaza Hotel and $500 sh spending money payable to Entrant and Model, (approximate prize value: $8,000), and one (1) Runner-up Prize of 00 cash payable to Entrant and Model for a romantic dinner for two (approximate prize value: $200). Prizes are valued U.S. currency. Prizes consist of only those items listed as part of the prize. No substitution of prize(s) permitted by nners. All prizes are awarded jointly to the Entrant and Model of the winning entries, and are not severable - prizes d obligations may not be assigned or transferred. Any change to the Entrant and/or Model of the winning entries will sult in disqualification and an alternate will be selected. Taxes on prize are the sole responsibility of winners. Any and expenses and/or items not specifically described as part of the prize are the sole responsibility of winners. Harlequin terprises Ltd. and D.L. Blair, Inc., their parents, affiliates, and subsidiaries are not responsible for errors in printing of ntest entries and/or game pieces. No responsibility is assumed for lost, stolen, late, illegible, incomplete, inaccurate, n-delivered, postage due or misdirected mail or entries. In the event of printing or other errors which may result in intended prize values or duplication of prizes, all affected game pieces or entries shall be null and void.

Winners will be notified by mail. For winners' list (available after March 31, 2004), send a self-addressed, stamped velope to: Harlequin Blaze Cover Model Search Contest 3569 Winners, P.O. Box 4200, Blair, NE 68009-4200, or er to the Harlequin website at www.blazecovermodel.com.

ntest sponsored by Harlequin Enterprises Ltd., P.O. Box 9042, Buffalo, NY 14269-9042.

HBCVRMODEL2

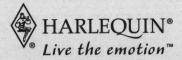

HARLEQUIN®
INTRIGUE®

presents another outstanding installment
in our bestselling series

COLORADO CONFIDENTIAL

**By day these agents are cowboys; by night they are
specialized government operatives. Men bound by love,
loyalty and the law—they've vowed to keep their
missions and identities confidential...**

August 2003
ROCKY MOUNTAIN MAVERICK
BY GAYLE WILSON

September 2003
SPECIAL AGENT NANNY
BY LINDA O. JOHNSTON

In **October**, look for an exciting short-story collection
featuring *USA TODAY* bestselling author
JASMINE CRESSWELL

November 2003
COVERT COWBOY
BY HARPER ALLEN

December 2003
A WARRIOR'S MISSION
BY RITA HERRON

PLUS
FIND OUT HOW IT ALL BEGAN
with three tie-in books from Harlequin Historicals,
starting January 2004

Available at your favorite retail outlet.

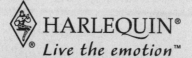

HARLEQUIN®
Live the emotion™

Visit us at www.eHarlequin.com

HICCAST